N

# FOOTBALL FURY

# FOOTBALL FURY

## By Steve Gelman

Illustrated by
Tracy Sugarman

Doubleday & Company, Inc.
Garden City, New York

F
G

Prepared by 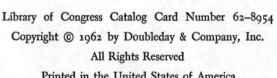 Rutledge Books

# CONTENTS

# FOOTBALL FURY

## chapter 1

# TIM BOSWELL, TACKLE

Tim Boswell braced himself for a crash. Coming straight at him, fast, was the biggest boy on the State University freshman football team. The boy had a football tucked under his arm and he was speeding with it toward the goal line. Only Tim stood in his way. "Well, it is all up to me this time," Tim said to himself. "Here goes."

Tim flung himself forward, but instead of grabbing ankles, Tim's hands grabbed air. The boy had dodged and was running across the goal line.

Tim kicked at the ground as he stood up. He felt alone and lost. What was the matter with him, forgetting simple things he had always been able to do on the football field? The warm September sun beat down on his back. His face was covered with sweat. The pads under his wet uniform seemed to weigh a ton. Tim had been a fullback, the power man on a football team, for as long as he could remember. Now he was playing tackle and he wasn't sure of what he was doing any more.

It was the third day of freshman football practice at State University. Tim took a deep breath as he heard Coach Butch Bronco's booming voice. "Get going," the coach said, "and play football. I want all of you moving together. Line up now and move off that line together."

Tim was playing on defense against other boys on the State University freshman team. They were all playing as hard as they could. They wanted to win starting positions on the team, and they knew that they would be measured by how well they played in practice.

Tim bent low and planted his feet firmly in the grass. He put his left arm in front of him, digging his fist into the dirt and bracing himself in the three-point position of a charging lineman. Behind him, Tim heard the command of the right line backer.

"Red dog right," the line backer barked.

In front of Tim, the State University freshman offense team put the football into play. Tim's team mate, the right line backer, crashed through the line in pursuit of the quarterback who had the ball. Tim ran along, too, thumping through the opposing players, and tackled the quarterback.

But the quarterback no longer had the ball.

Tim rolled over on his back, stretched the full length of his six feet, three inches, and smashed his fist into the sweet-smelling grass. As he dragged his 220-pound body to a standing position, the player with the ball—the boy Tim had not tackled—was over the goal line.

Touchdown! It was a touchdown for the other team, the second one in five minutes. And Tim had made them both possible.

Coach Bronco got up from his bench, his face flushed with anger. "Boswell," he yelled, his booming voice shaking. "Boswell, get over here!"

Tim ran toward the coach. He was so nervous he stumbled on his way to the coach's bench. Tim looked at Coach Bronco. "His face is almost as red as his shirt," Tim thought.

"Did you hear that signal?" the coach asked. "Did you hear the signal for a red dog right?"

Tim nodded. He could not take his eyes off Coach Bronco's angry face. "He looks as if he might explode into a million pieces," Tim thought. "He looks as if he might blow up this second."

"Did you hear the signal, Boswell?" Coach Bronco asked again.

Tim chewed hard on the blade of grass in his mouth. He looked at the gold whistle hanging from Coach Bronco's neck. "Yes, sir," Tim said. "I heard the signal."

"Then why weren't you in position? You were not supposed to charge the quarterback. On a red dog play,

the line backer charges. A tackle—and you are a tackle, Boswell—does not charge. You are supposed to cover the line backer's position. Instead, *you* charged, and they scored a touchdown because the man with the ball ran right through the space you left open for him."

It was quiet. It was so quiet that Tim thought he could hear his heart thumping. All the other players were standing still, not making a sound. Tim stared harder at Coach Bronco's gleaming whistle. They were all listening to Coach Bronco as he yelled at Tim.

"This is football, Boswell," Coach Bronco said. "We play it with eleven men. Every man has his job to do.

If one man doesn't do his job, the whole team suffers. Ten men did their jobs right on that play. One man— you—did his job wrong, and they scored a touchdown."

Tim bit hard on his lower lip. He could not get used to being bawled out by his coach. Ever since Tim could remember, he had been hearing cheers, not complaints. They had been loud, clear cheers that cut sharply through the autumn air. They were the cheers of football crowds, hoarse and happy, ringing out his name. Saturday after Saturday, Tim Boswell had run like the wind for the goal line and glory. He had been the big star at Grand High School, scoring touchdowns, winning games.

Only a year ago, Tim remembered, Coach Bronco had been among the people praising him. Tim had offers from 20 colleges to play football for them in return for which they would help pay his college expenses, but Coach Bronco had convinced him to come to State U.

Tim remembered Coach Bronco's words. "If you play for State," Coach Bronco had said, "you will be only 100 miles from home. Your friends, your parents and your kid brother can come up to see you. Besides, we are going to have top teams for the next couple of years and you will have a chance to become famous. Football scouts from the professional teams will see you. Everybody in the country will know who you are."

Tim would never forget those words. He remembered every word of the conversation. He could see Coach Bronco as the coach looked on that day a year ago. He was dressed in a blue suit, and not wearing a red shirt as he was today. Tim remembered that the coach had been sitting in the big living room chair, smiling and laughing. Tim thought, too, about what his father had asked Coach Bronco.

"Forget football for a moment," Tim's father had said. "Is State U. a football factory like those other schools we read about? Will Tim only play football or will he get an education, too?"

Coach Bronco had sat up straight in the chair. "Of course he will get an education. Before I came here, I checked Tim's high school marks. His marks are good. If they were not, I could not ask him to come to State U. A football player can't even play at State U. unless he gets good grades. Tim will get an education and he will become a star football player, too. He can be an all-around star—in the classroom and on the football field."

Tim remembered those words as he stood now in front of Coach Bronco. The blade of grass did a dance in Tim's mouth. Things certainly were not the way Coach Bronco had said they would be. The very first day Tim had reported for freshman football practice, things had begun to change.

Tim thought about that first day. It seemed as though it had been months ago. Tim and the other players had sat in Indian style on the grass, their legs crossed in front of them, as Coach Bronco greeted them.

"A lot of you boys were big stars in high school,"

Bronco had said in his booming voice. "But your high school records mean nothing here. You are first year football players. State U. freshman football players. My job is to train you for next year, when you will be playing for the regular team. Now you are here to work hard. You all rate the same."

Then each player had had a private talk with the coach.

"Boswell," Bronco had said to Tim, "you were a fullback in high school, a good fullback. We know that. But we have another fellow on the freshman team who was a fullback. He is Len Hawkins. He played fullback for Rambler High and he is going to be the fullback on our team. We need tackles, so we are switching your position. At State U., you are going to be a tackle. I think you can make the change, Boswell. I saw you play in high school. You are a natural athlete and I think you will make a good man on the line. Now, let's see what you can do."

Tim had been playing tackle for three days. There was so much to learn at the new position that he could not do anything right. It seemed as though he were standing before the coach every five minutes to be bawled out.

"Okay, Boswell," the coach said. "Let's see if you can do it right tomorrow." Coach Bronco reached for the whistle and blew three shrill blasts. "Okay, team," he shouted. "Practice is over."

Tim ripped off his helmet. The cool air felt good on his crew-cut brown hair. He watched Coach Bronco's short, heavy body disappear into the locker room. The State U. freshman players joked and laughed as they ran toward the showers. Tim walked behind them, taking short, slow steps. Suddenly, he was pushed forward as one of the players thumped him on the back.

It was Chuck Denton. Chuck had been the quarterback at Grand High when Tim had played fullback there. They had been best friends and now they were room mates at State U. "Forget it," Chuck said. "Everybody makes mistakes. You will learn. After all, you are playing a new position."

Tim threw his helmet into the air and caught it with one hand. "I want to learn, Chuck," he said.

Chuck ran his hand through his black hair. His eyes grew dark. He stopped walking and turned to Tim. "It's not fair, Tim," Chuck said.

"What is not fair?"

"What they are doing to you here, making you switch positions. You are every bit as good a fullback as Hawkins. As a matter of fact, I think you are better. What a deal! When we move up to the regular team next year, everybody in the state is going to hear about Hawkins. But who is going to hear about you? The fullbacks get all the glory, but the tackles work just as hard and nobody knows about it. The tackles block for the fullbacks and take all the knocks and nobody cheers for them. The tackles do all the tough work that no one notices."

Tim didn't say anything as he walked into the locker

room with Chuck. He moved to his locker almost in a dream. Clouds of steam from the shower room drifted over his head.

Tim sat down in front of his locker. He pulled the shoes from his feet and dropped them with a thump. He hung his helmet on the edge of the bench and stood up, peeling off his green jersey. Slowly he took off his shoulder pads and, as he did so, he heard the snap of a towel behind him. He turned and looked up.

Billy Wilson, the left end, was doing a dance on top of the bench. Billy wasn't dancing a regular dance, like the fox trot. He was dancing as they do in the cowboy movies when a fellow with a pistol starts firing bullets

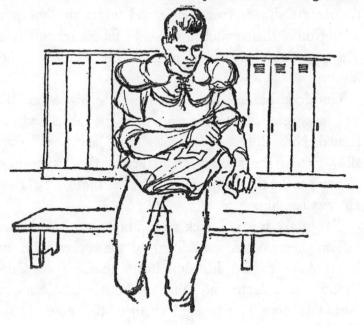

at another fellow's feet. But Billy was not dancing away from bullets. He was dancing away from a snapping towel. Jack Gerard, the stumpy guard, was on the bench, too, snapping a wet towel at Billy's feet.

"Dance, boy," Jack shouted.

Billy jumped.

Jack snapped the towel, coming close to Billy's bare toes. "Dance again, man."

Billy danced and Jack snapped. The freshman football players gathered around the bench. They were all laughing. All but Tim. Tim tried to smile but he couldn't. He took off the rest of his uniform and wrapped a towel around his waist. Taking his own time, he walked into the steamy shower room. He stood under the hot water a long time, then switched the cold faucet on full force. The cold water made his skin tingle, but it couldn't cheer him up.

Tim dried himself and walked back to his locker. Billy and Jack were still at their game, but the tables had been turned. Now Billy had the towel and Jack was dancing. Billy chased the stumpy guard across the locker room. "Your turn, pal," Billy yelled. "Move those feet. Fast!" He was laughing.

"Hey, take it easy," Jack said, jumping out of the way.

Tim dressed and walked out of the locker room and went alone toward his dormitory, thinking of Coach Bronco's complaints and thinking about what Chuck had said. The more Tim thought about it, the more unhappy he became. Chuck's words kept running through his mind. That night, after he said good night to Chuck, he was unable to sleep. He tossed in his bed, thinking, "The fullbacks get all the glory, and the tackles get all the tough work."

## chapter 2

# A PROMISE TO GET EVEN

Every muscle in Tim's body ached. It was the second week of practice and Tim was so tired that he felt he would never be able to last out the season. He walked slowly up the dormitory steps.

It hadn't been like this in high school. There, practice had been fun, and afterward there had always been time for a soda with the gang. But now, studies were piling up. In high school, studying had taken two hours a night and if he had any problems with his school work his dad had always been there to help him. Now he was on his own and there was never enough time!

Tim climbed the last step and walked down the hall, whistling softly. The hall was quiet. He had been the first one to leave the locker room, so the usual sounds coming from the rooms of the other players were missing.

He opened the door to his room and threw his books on the large brown desk underneath the two State U. pennants. He raised the window to let in cool air. The tired feeling would not leave. "If I lie down for five minutes," he said to himself, "I will feel more like studying." He had a test in history the next day and he knew he had no time to waste. It meant he had to study for an hour before dinner and for at least another two hours later.

Tim opened the buttons of his sport shirt and flopped on his bed.

The next thing he knew, Chuck was shaking him awake. "What's the matter?" Chuck asked. "Don't you want dinner?"

"Dinner? Is it time for dinner?" Tim asked. He rubbed his eyes and ran his hand down the side of his wrinkled shirt.

"Dinner is almost over," Chuck said. "There are only a couple of fellows left at the training table. If you run down now, maybe you can still get something to eat, but you had better hurry."

Tim went to the sink and splashed some water on his face. He smoothed down his shirt and pulled a comb from his pocket and combed his hair.

"Why are you doing that?" Chuck asked. "Your hair is so short you can't comb it anyway."

Tim laughed as he ran the comb through his hair one

more time. "Now," he said, "off to the dining room."

Tim threw on his sports jacket. "Thanks for waking me, Chuck," he said. He ran down the dormitory steps two at a time, and rushed through the dining room door toward the training table. Only Len Hawkins was still there.

As Tim reached the table, Hawkins looked up and laughed. "What's the matter, Boswell?" the big fullback asked. "You look as if you just woke up."

"I did," Tim said. "My whole schedule is fouled up now."

"What do you mean?" Hawkins asked.

"I will never be able to study long enough to pass the history test tomorrow," Tim said.

Hawkins laughed. "Don't be a sap," he said. "You can pass the test without studying. Don't knock yourself out. If you play the angles right, school work is a snap." Hawkins winked.

"What do you mean?"

"You are in my history class, right? Well, I know a fellow who takes the same class in the morning and, last week, we got the same test he got. He took the test in the morning and we took it in the afternoon. The same test, get it? All we have to do is meet him and check out the answers. No extra studying. It's a breeze."

Hawkins winked again and Tim picked up a tray. "I will have to think about it," Tim said. "See you tomorrow morning."

Tim walked to the food counter and piled two slabs of roast beef and a mound of green peas on a plate. He put the plate on his tray and put a glass of milk next to it. He ate quickly and went back to his room. He thought about Hawkins' plan. Right then, it seemed like a good idea. Then he thought about what his father had said to Coach Bronco.

"I am not here to be put through a football factory," Tim thought as he walked into his room. "I am here to learn as well as to play football. I play football fair and square, and I will take my tests the same way. Hawkins can do what he wants. I am going to study."

Tim took off his sports jacket. As he walked by Chuck's bed, he poked him in the ribs. Chuck jumped up and dropped his book. "Hey, you made me lose my place," Chuck said. "You get any dinner?"

"Roast beef that was cooked too long, but I ate it so fast I couldn't tell the difference."

"Serves you right for sleeping in the afternoon," Chuck said. "Now shut up and let me study."

"Don't worry about me," Tim said. "I have plenty of studying to do myself. I will be studying long after you are asleep. I have a history test tomorrow that is going to be a tough one."

Tim sat down at the desk and picked up his book. He opened it and began reading, whistling softly.

"Cut that out," Chuck said. "You know you can't carry a tune. Your whistling drives me bats."

"Okay, okay," Tim said. "No more whistling. No more talking."

Soon Tim's desk lamp was the only light on in the room. Chuck was sleeping and snoring, but it didn't bother Tim. He was too busy with history. Finally, Tim looked at his wrist watch. "Past midnight," he yawned. "I hope I know enough to pass."

The next afternoon, Tim sat in the combination chair and desk in the history class room. He tried to make himself comfortable but his body was cramped in the small chair.

There were ten questions on the test and Tim knew seven of them—enough to pass, but not enough to get a very good mark. He left the room happy that he had passed, and happy that he had not cheated. But he was sorry he had not done better.

In the locker room, Tim dressed quickly. He put on his shoes and thumped down the hall carrying his helmet in his hand. As he walked to the field, he saw Billy Wilson shove Jack Gerard into a pile of leaves. Jack grabbed up a handful of leaves and flung them at Bill. Then the chunky Gerard leaped up and chased Bill on to the field.

Tim laughed. "What a pair of characters," he said to Chuck, who had come up beside him.

Tim saw Hawkins walk out of the locker room. "I wonder how he did on the test?" Tim thought. But before

Tim had a chance to ask the big fullback, Coach Bronco blew three sharp blasts on the whistle. The players ran on to the field and stood in front of the coach.

"Everybody take four laps around the field," Coach Bronco boomed. "I want to see you run as fast as you can. I want to see your tongues hanging out. Now, start moving!"

Tim and Chuck took off around the field. Their shoes cut into the soft grass, digging up dirt. Tim ran easily, pacing himself, and Chuck did the same. Billy Wilson ran full steam and Jack Gerard came along slowly, the way slow-moving guards generally do. By the third lap, Tim and Chuck had caught up to Billy. Right behind them were Hawkins and Sammy Swift, the fast halfback.

Coach Bronco's booming voice cut through the sounds of the heavy breathing. "Let's run. Let's move. Come on, Gerard, you are running like a snail."

Tim turned into the final lap, passing Chuck and Wilson. He ran with smooth strides, eating up the yards. About ten yards from the end, Sammy Swift and Hawkins came up to him. Swift shot past Tim, but Tim turned on enough speed to beat Hawkins. Chuck came up next and draped an arm around Tim's shoulders. "See what I mean?" Chuck said. "You are faster than Len Hawkins any day."

Tim bounced up and down, doing exercises in time to Coach Bronco's commands. When the exercises were over, it was time for game practice. Tim lined up at tackle

with the defense. He tugged at his helmet and slapped his shoulder pads as he settled into his new three-point position. He listened as Chuck, who was playing quarterback for the offense, called the signals. He watched Chuck bend over behind the center and take the ball on a short, direct snap. Tim thumped past the opposing lineman and drove into the backfield. Chuck handed the ball to Hawkins, charging hard into the line from his fullback position. Hawkins came directly at Tim, knees high, head low, the football held fast in his arms.

Tim dived forward and grabbed Hawkins' shoulders.

Right line backer Cliff Zanger jumped on Hawkins, too. The big fullback fell to the ground as players from both teams piled on top of him. Tim was at the bottom of the pile, breathing hard. He felt a sharp pain in his right side. Tim was sure Hawkins had hit him. As the boys got up from the pile, Tim felt a fist smashing into his stomach. Then he felt an elbow in his cheek. Only Hawkins could have done that, Tim knew. But why?

Play after play, whenever Tim and Hawkins ended up in the same pile, Tim felt fists smashing him and elbows poking him. He couldn't understand it. Tim knew that Hawkins had never played dirty against him before.

Tim walked to the locker room with Cliff Zanger afterward, and they talked about the practice game.

"Was it my imagination?" Tim said. "I could swear that Hawkins was after me today."

"I don't know," Cliff said. "I couldn't tell. If he was hitting you when we were piled up, you are the only one who could tell."

Tim stripped the paper from a stick of gum and stuck the gum in his mouth.

Suddenly a voice snapped, "You look like a calf, Boswell, chewing on your cud."

It was Hawkins, and Tim knew immediately that the big fullback was not being funny. Hawkins was angry. Tim looked down and saw that Hawkins' hands were doubled into fists.

Tim rubbed his hand through his hair, his face dark

and puzzled. "I want to talk to you, Boswell," Hawkins said. "I want to talk things over with you."

"What things?" Tim asked.

Suddenly, three shrill whistle blasts cut through the air. Coach Bronco was standing in front of the locker room.

In a few seconds all the State U. freshman football players were standing in front of the coach.

"Nothing very important, boys," the coach said. "I just want to tell you that practice will be at 3:30 tomorrow instead of at three. I will post a notice on the bulletin board, but I wanted to make sure you all knew."

The boys ran on into the locker room.

"Okay," Hawkins said in a low, angry voice, as he

and Tim stood side by side at their lockers. "How did you find out?"

"Find out what?" Tim said.

Hawkins pulled himself up to his full six-feet, four inches and placed his face inches away from Tim's. Their eyes were almost level. Hawkins' eyes were burning with anger. "You found out that old Grosston was changing the test this time."

Tim stared straight at Hawkins. "I didn't know anything about it," Tim said.

"Oh, yeah? Then how come you didn't show up to find out what questions he asked on the morning test?"

"Because I decided I wanted to study. I decided I didn't want it your way, that's why." Tim's face was flushed.

"I don't believe you," Hawkins said. "The least you could have done was to let me in on it. I know I didn't pass that test and old Grosston is the kind of professor who would be glad to give a football player a bad mark. You know darn well that he could get me thrown off the team. But that would suit you, wouldn't it? If I were thrown off the team, then *you* might be the fullback. That's what you want, right?"

"Hawkins," Tim said. "You are all wrong. I didn't know a thing about the test."

Hawkins smashed his fist into his palm. He stared into Tim's eyes. He smacked his palm again. "Just wait, Boswell," he said. "My chance will come to pay you back."

## chapter 3

# THE MISTAKE

Tim was wide awake. A cool, fresh wind blew through the windows of the dormitory room. "That wind is going to help our kicking," Tim thought, as he lay in bed propped up on an elbow.

He looked over at Chuck's bed and there was Chuck, propped up on one elbow, wide awake, too. Tim laughed, and leaped out of bed.

"I thought you were sleeping," he said.

"I thought *you* were sleeping," Chuck said. He swung his legs over the side of the bed and sat up.

"Who can sleep today?" Tim said. "First game of the season. This is what I have been waiting for."

"Me, too," Chuck said. "But I will tell you one thing. Burton is going to be a tough team to beat. I would feel a lot better about our chances of winning if you were playing fullback today. You always scored the touchdowns when we needed them in high school."

Tim looked out the window. He stared at the blue sky. It was the kind of weather that pepped a fellow up, the kind of weather, Tim thought, that gave a fullback pep to run as fast as he possibly could. This was the kind of day that put snap into a fullback's hard charges up the middle of the field. He had always run with power and speed in weather like this.

"But I am not a fullback any more," he said to himself. "I am a tackle, and maybe I will be able to block and tackle better too in this kind of weather. Sure. Why not? If I always played well at fullback when the air was cool, why can't I play well at tackle?"

He walked to the sink and brushed his teeth. Chuck came up behind him. Tim began to comb his hair.

"Switch places with me," Chuck said. "You can look into the mirror over my head. I can't see anything but your back."

They switched. Tim towered over Chuck. Chuck was lean and strong, but even at five feet, eleven inches and 185 pounds, he always seemed small when he stood next to Tim.

Tim and Chuck dressed slowly. They sat on their beds and talked, but neither had much to say. Their minds were too much on the game. It was hard to think of anything but football the day of the first game. They left the room at seven o'clock and went downstairs for breakfast.

Tim had never seen the fellows so quiet at the training table. Jack Gerard told Billy Wilson to turn around and look at the door and, while Billy was looking the other way, Jack switched his empty milk glass for Billy's full one. But otherwise there was no fooling around. Even Len Hawkins was quiet.

At 8:30, the freshman football players began walking toward the locker room. The game was scheduled for eleven o'clock on the practice field. The freshman team could not play in the big stadium because the varsity team was going to play there in the afternoon.

Tim, Chuck and Cliff Zanger walked together. Cliff was carrying a copy of the State U. student newspaper. In it there was a story about the game. Above the story were the words: STATE FRESHMEN FAVORED TO BEAT BURTON.

"I sure hope we *can* beat them," Cliff said. "I understand that Burton College has some really fine players this year. They have some of the best freshmen in the country."

"The paper says it depends on Hawkins," Cliff said, "and that Hawkins has looked so good in practice that Burton will not be able to stop him."

"We will beat them," Tim said. "I know we will. We have the power."

"What else does the paper say?" Chuck asked.

Cliff stopped and tried to keep the glare of the sun out of his eyes as he read. "It says that a fellow named Chuck Denton has looked mighty sharp at quarterback," Cliff said. "It says that this Chuck Denton is very good at passing."

Chuck stuck his chest out. "How do you like that?" he said, laughing. "I am great at passing! What does it say about Tim?"

Cliff looked again. "Nothing in the story," he said. "You are just listed to start, Tim. It says 'Billy Wilson, right end, Tim Boswell, right tackle.'"

Tim whistled softly. It had not been like that in high school. In high school all the papers had put him on the front page. People had always said that Tim Boswell was the fullback who could not be stopped.

The boys walked across the grass and into the locker

room. Their uniforms were piled on the narrow benches in front of the lockers. Tim picked up his uniform shirt, white with green letters. It was a game uniform, washed and sparkling clean. Quite a difference from the old, battered practice uniforms. Tim stared at his number. It was number 77, a tackle's number. Tim remembered reading that Red Grange, one of the greatest running backs of all time, wore number 77 when he played for the University of Illinois. He felt proud that he was wearing the same number. Tim knew that these days numbers are given out according to positions. The back-field men wear numbers from 1 to 40, the ends usually wear numbers in the 80s, the tackles get numbers in the 70s, the guards wear numbers in the 60s and the centers wear numbers in the 50s. "In the old days," Tim thought, "it didn't matter."

Tim stripped off his school clothes and began to put on his uniform. He looked across the locker room. There was Coach Bronco. The coach was wearing a blue suit, not a red shirt. He didn't even have the whistle around his neck. He was dressed up for the game.

When Tim was dressed, he sat quietly in front of his locker. Billy was having trouble with his shoulder pads and Hawkins was helping him, talking in a loud voice. "What's the matter, Billy boy," Hawkins asked. "Don't be too nervous to put on your pads. We are going in there to win. Old Len Hawkins will see to that. I will score so many touchdowns you won't be able to count them."

Suddenly Coach Bronco spoke. "Okay, gang," he said. "Let's get together."

The players gathered around the coach. "No more talk from me today," the coach said. "Just remember everything I taught you in practice. Play *together*. Team work is the secret. Every man do his job, and we will win."

Coach Bronco waved to the door and the players ran out. Tim was first man on the field and he began kicking his legs up and down. The other players did the same. Across the field, the Burton team was already done with

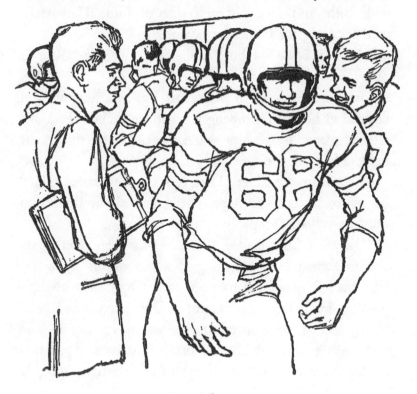

exercises and the players were running through passing drills, throwing and catching the ball. Some of the Burton players were standing at the goal line, taking turns kicking, while other players were standing 40 yards away, catching the kicks and, with each catch, running a few feet with the ball.

Chuck ran out on the field and called for the State U. players to line up in front of him. Chuck had been picked as the State U. game captain and it was his job to lead the exercises. Tim stood in front of Chuck, with Billy and Jack on each side of him. They stood erect, waiting for Chuck to begin.

"Run in place," Chuck hollered. "Let's go! Run in place!"

Tim began to run in place, his legs churning up and down, but he wasn't moving forward or backward. Chuck ran in place, too, as he called out, "Left, right, left, right, left, right."

The longer the State U. players ran, the faster Chuck began to call out the steps, until, after about three minutes, he yelled, "Stop."

"Okay," Chuck called, "touch your toes. Let's go."

Tim leaned over, touching the toes of his right foot with his left hand, the toes of his left foot with his right hand. Chuck began to count, "One, two, one, two," slowly at first, then speeding up. Tim was swinging back and forth so fast he almost lost his balance. Each time he leaned over to touch the toes of his right foot, he caught sight of Coach Bronco, who was standing on the sidelines, watching.

"Let's work on your blocking muscles," Chuck commanded as soon as the toe-touching exercise was over. "Blocking drill."

The players split up into pairs. Tim stood, facing Billy. Using their shoulders, they hit each other sharply, but not with too much force, getting themselves loose.

When the players bent low in their three-point position, Tim dug in and drove his body straight ahead at Billy. He moved Billy back, inch by inch, step by step. Then it was Billy's turn. Billy rushed forward, and Tim felt his shoulder pad hit him in the chest and he fell back as Billy drove into him.

Seconds later, Billy smacked Tim so hard that Tim tumbled over flat on his back. "Gee, sorry," Billy said. "I shouldn't have hit you so hard."

Tim stumbled to his feet. He was smiling. "That's okay, Billy," he said. "That's okay. Just hit those Burton guys as hard as that in the game. That's the kind of blocking we need if we are going to win."

When the State U. boys were finished with their exercises, they lined up for their kicking and passing practice. As they did, Tim heard Coach Bronco's booming voice.

"Boswell," the coach yelled. "Come here!"

Tim walked over. Why was Coach Bronco calling him over—alone? What had he done wrong now?

"Boswell," Bronco said. "I want you to remember what I have been telling you about blocking. Hit your man low when you block and make sure you keep him down."

The words were ringing in Tim's ears as the game began. Blocking was a new part of football for Tim. In high school, he had seldom blocked for the runners. When he was not running with the ball himself, he had usually been charging into the line as though he had the ball, in order to get the players on the opposing team to tackle him while another boy ran for a big gain. He had never had to think about blocking low, the way line men must to clear a path for the player who had the ball.

Tim's blocking had improved since he had begun practicing with the State U. freshman team, but he still was not good at it. Now, as the game started, he missed blocks in the first quarter, but State was able to hold off any scoring. At the end of three quarters the score was nothing to nothing but, as the fourth quarter began, Burton's left halfback broke loose for a long gain down the side of the field.

Though Tim and Chuck took off after him, Tim knew he was too far behind ever to catch the Burton boy. Hawkins and halfback Jug Lary were after him, too. Tim heard the Burton coach yelling, "Touchdown, touchdown! Run! Run! Run!" But it was not a touchdown. With a burst of speed, Jug caught up and hauled the Burton halfback down from behind.

The ball was placed on the State U. 10-yard line. Tim dug in at the line. On defense, State U. played with five men on the line, two line backers and four backs for defense. Jack, who played a guard on offense, played in the middle of the line on defense. Tim played on one side of Jack, while the second tackle played on Jack's other side. Billy Wilson played at end next to Tim.

Three times the Burton backs crashed into State U.'s line, and three times they were turned back with no gain. Jack made two tackles, Tim made one. Tim was proud of himself as he lined up to stop Burton's final try. The sweat was pouring down his face, but he was not tired. He never felt tired in a tough, close football game.

Burton did not try to run again. Instead, the Burton quarterback kneeled down six yards behind the center. The Burton fullback stood farther back, kicking his leg into the air to get his muscles loose. It would be a try for a field goal. The Burton fullback kicked the ball with a good solid thump. It flew into the air, flopping end over end, straight between the goal posts and over the cross-bars. Burton was ahead, 3–0.

The State U. players got into their positions, ready to receive the kick off from Burton. Tim glanced at the large clock at the end of the field. There was still time to win, plenty of time.

Quickly Burton kicked off to State, all the players moving with the kick off. Sammy Swift grabbed the ball

and ran with it all the way to the Burton 25-yard line. But there the drive ended.

Back and forth went the football. First Burton kicked. Then State kicked. Then Burton kicked again. The last kick was a bad one for Burton. It skidded off the side of the fullback's foot and went out of bounds on the Burton 15-yard line.

Tim jumped up and down. Chuck thumped Cliff on the back. What a break! There was time now for only one or two plays, but fifteen yards was not far to go.

The State team had been waiting for just such a chance.

State took time out. The players raced back and stood shoulder to shoulder in a circle, listening to Chuck. Chuck's voice was low and firm. He looked at Tim, at Jug, at Billy. Last, he looked at Hawkins. "Mouse trap four," Chuck said clearly. It was State's trap play.

The State U. team broke sharply from the circle, lining up in a straight T. Seven men were up on the line. Chuck stood directly behind the center, close enough to be bent over him. Behind Chuck was fullback

Hawkins and on each side of Hawkins was one of the State U. halfbacks.

"Set! Down! Blue four! Got it!"

Chuck's voice cut through the quiet, barking out the signals. "One! Two! Three . . . ! One! Two! Three . . . !"

The ball was snapped. Chuck had it in his hands. He faded back fast as if he were throwing a pass. He faded and faked, faded and faked. Tim and the other State linemen followed the mouse trap play. They let the other team charge right past them.

The four Burton front linemen ran in. Tim raced out to block the left line backer. Tim knew what was going on behind him. Chuck was waiting until the four Burton men were right on top of him. Then, suddenly, Chuck handed the ball off to Hawkins.

The big fullback tucked the football into his stomach. He put his head down and raced forward, rushing toward the goal line only fifteen yards away. Tim was ahead of him. Tim had to block out the left line backer. He rushed forward and hit the line backer, but the player did not go down. Instead, he came back at Tim, hitting him hard and throwing him back. Someone crashed into Tim. It was Hawkins. The Burton line backer had pushed Tim into Hawkins' path. The ball, knocked from Hawkins' hands, went flying into the air as the boys tangled. The big fullback, unable to get free, fell to the ground, short of the goal line.

A loud shot echoed across the field. It was the gun cracking out the end of the game. Tim lay on the ground. Suddenly, with the game over, all his muscles hurt. The defeat hurt even more. He stood up slowly.

Tim was the last man to come into the quiet locker room. He smelled the rubbing alcohol that the team manager was slapping on the sore bodies of his team mates. Tim looked at the floor. He did not want to talk to anybody.

But Hawkins wanted to talk to him. The big fullback stood right in Tim's path. "You lost that game for us, Boswell," Hawkins said.

Tim looked up. He saw Coach Bronco standing only five feet away. He knew the coach was listening. He also knew that Hawkins wanted the coach to listen. "Just one little block," Hawkins was saying. "Just one little block and I would have been through for the touchdown. One little block from you, that's all I needed to win the game."

Tim stared at the floor. He could not lift his eyes to face Hawkins. Tim knew Hawkins had no right to yell at him. "If I really lost the game for the team," Tim thought, "then Coach Bronco would tell me."

At last Tim looked up. "Get out of my way," he said quickly.

"*Make* me get out of the way, Boswell," Hawkins said, and took a step toward Tim. Hawkins smiled. His face was smeared with dirt from the field and it loomed dark and dirty in front of Tim.

In an instant Coach Bronco was between the two boys. The coach's face was puffed with anger. His blue suit was creased. His eyes were drawn. "Hawkins," he said. "Get into that shower room. Boswell, get over to your locker. You guys cut it out or you are both off the team. Around here we have team spirit. We win if we play together, not if we fight."

Tim began to walk away and so did Hawkins. But Coach Bronco tapped Tim's shoulder. Tim turned. "Boswell," Bronco said, his voice almost a whisper. "You hit that man high. If you had blocked him low, we would have won that game."

## chapter 4

# A NEW FRIEND

Tim was standing alone on a small hill that looked over the State University grounds. He had twenty minutes to himself before reporting for football practice. Below him, the gray stone buildings rose high toward the sky. From where Tim was standing, the green vines covering the buildings looked like spots of paint.

He turned and looked down the hill toward the football field. "That is the field where the great State U. teams played, where they played against Red Grange and Doc Blanchard and Glenn Davis. And here I am, playing on the same field."

A voice with a thick German sound cut into Tim's thoughts. "What are you thinking about, young man?"

Tim turned. Standing in front of him was a small man,

45

dressed in shabby clothes and carrying a rake. He knew the man was Hans Luger, the college grounds keeper. Tim had heard some of the players talking about him. "Hans, the Nut," they had called him.

Tim had once asked Coach Bronco about Hans.

"Hans is the chief grounds keeper," the coach had told him. "He usually comes around the practice field some time during the day. When he was young, he was a fine athlete in Germany. But he was hurt seriously in a game and couldn't play any more. It nearly broke

46

his heart. He came to America and drifted around the country for a long time until finally he got the job here at State U. He has been here for many, many years."

Now Tim was meeting Hans in person. "I am sorry," Tim said. "What did you say?"

"I was wondering, young man, what you were thinking about."

"Oh, nothing much."

"You thinking about football, maybe? I see you play football. I see you running pretty fast all the time."

"You think I run fast?" Tim said. "That's about all I seem to be able to do any more."

"What you mean?" Hans said.

"Do you know much about football?" Tim asked. "Yes."

"Well, I used to be a fullback, a good fullback. But when I got to State U., Coach Bronco switched my position. He made me a tackle. And now the only times I get a chance to run are when you see me in practice."

Hans looked at Tim with friendly eyes. "I know you are a tackle. Tackles are important men on football teams. But I know, too, that Coach Bronco is no fool. I am sure, young man, that he believes you are a good enough player to be great no matter where you are playing."

"Well, maybe so," Tim said, "but from the way he keeps yelling at me I am not so sure."

"He is maybe wanting you to try harder. He is maybe wanting you to try so hard to play tackle that you will

47

forget you ever played fullback and think only of blocking and tackling."

Tim was silent for a minute. He knew there was another
reason why he was not doing well as a tackle. "I really
haven't forgotten about the cheers," he thought. It was
not easy to forget the glory that was his when, as his
high school's fullback, he raced down the field, the
ball held firmly in the crook of his arm, for touchdown
after touchdown, the crowd cheering him on.

Tim reached down and scooped up some leaves. "I
suppose I am just going to have to try hard to forget that
I was ever a fullback," he said to Hans. "But the fellow
who is fullback now—Len Hawkins—is not going to make
it easy for me. Every time I make a mistake he lets me hear
about it after the game. If he had good blocking and good
tackling he could score the touchdowns, he says. We lose
a game or do badly in practice and he is right there, putting the blame on me or some other player." Tim crumbled
the leaves he held in his hand and let the pieces fall to
the ground.

Hans smiled and his wrinkled face seemed to crack
like leather. "You are a smart young man," he said. "Why
would Hawkins always want to blame things on somebody else?"

"I don't know," Tim said.

"One reason would be, maybe, he is not so sure of
himself after all," Hans said.

Tim thought about this for a while, not certain what

Hans meant. "Maybe that is it," he said. "Maybe Hawkins is really scared, playing fullback. So afraid he will make a mistake that he would like to make the rest of us look as though it is we who are always wrong. That way, if he makes a mistake, he can always say 'So what! Everybody else does too.'"

Hans ran his hand back along his bald head. "You are smart boy," Hans said. "You forget about Hawkins and you forget about fullback. You learn to play tackle. You think about that."

Tim smiled, then suddenly he frowned. He looked at his wrist watch. "I am late for practice. Nice meeting you, Hans, but I have to run. Coach Bronco really boils when anyone is late."

Tim darted down the hill, running toward the football field. He turned once and saw Hans waving after him with his rake. "Old Hans has more sense than he is given credit for," Tim thought. Then, fast as he had ever run for a touchdown, Tim flew toward the locker room.

Tim dressed quickly and ran out on the field. As he came out, he heard Coach Bronco's whistle. "Okay," Bronco boomed. "No more exercises. Let's practice."

The freshman football players ran toward Coach Bronco. Tim ran with them, moving into the center of the crowd beside Chuck. "Where have you been?" Chuck said.

"I was talking," Tim said.

"Talking?"

"Yes."

49

Coach Bronco's voice cut through the noise of the chattering players.

"We are going to learn a new play today," Coach Bronco said. "It is the kind of play we can try only once in a game, but when it works, it works for long gains. You can surprise the other team with it the first time, but after that they will be watching for it." Coach Bronco rubbed his hands along his red shirt.

"We are going to learn the end-around pass play," Coach Bronco said. "We are lucky that we have an end who can make it work. Billy Wilson can pass and that is exactly what we need for this play—an end who can throw the ball."

Coach Bronco lined up the starting freshman team. They fell into the line-up for offense—a straight T. Tim set himself at tackle, with Jack Gerard, the guard, and Billy, the end, on either side of him. Chuck lined up at quarterback, behind Cliff Zanger, who played center on offense. Hawkins was at fullback directly behind Chuck. Jug Lary and Sammy Swift were the halfbacks. Coach Bronco explained the play. Tim was excited when he heard it. He liked to learn new plays, and the end-around pass play, Tim decided, was a dandy. This was the kind of work-out he liked best.

"Everybody understand it?" Bronco said.

"Got it, Coach," the players yelled.

"Good. Let's run it off. Second team, get out there on defense."

The practice was on. Tim's team did not run the end-around pass play right away. They wanted to use it as a surprise. First, they ran a straight fullback smash and Hawkins gained three yards. Then Chuck called for the mouse trap four and behind a fine block by Tim, Hawkins gained five more yards. "Good blocking, Tim," Sammy Swift said. "That's the way to knock them down."

Chuck signaled for silence. He spoke softly. "End-around pass play," he said. "Let's make it work."

The players ran to line up. Tim bent low in his three-point position. Chuck barked out the signals. "Set! Down! Blue white! Got it! One! Two . . . !"

Cliff snapped the ball. Chuck grabbed it. Tim pushed forward. He blocked the defensive end, getting him out of the play. Sammy Swift came around Chuck and Chuck faked handing him the ball. Sammy kept moving, picking up speed as he ran without the ball down the field. Chuck faded back.

Billy circled from his end position and ran into the backfield, cutting around Hawkins, who blocked out the defensive right line backer. Billy moved behind Chuck and Chuck thrust the football into his hands. Running toward the line, Billy suddenly stopped and flung the ball far down the field. The ball flew perfectly and at the 10-yard line, it came down. Sammy Swift, running full steam, made an over-the-shoulder catch and raced into the end zone for a touchdown.

Sammy flung the ball into the air. Billy and Chuck

pounded each other on the back. Tim and Jack picked themselves up off the ground and ran up the field, shouting. Coach Bronco blew three shrill blasts on his whistle.

"Great! Just great!" Coach Bronco said. "That is exactly what team work is. Every man did his job, and we scored. That is team work. Good going."

Twice more that afternoon the team worked the end-around pass play for touchdowns. They ran into the locker room after practice, pleased with their work. "Boy, will that work great in a real game!" Tim said. "Remember, we were working it today against fellows on our own team who know the play. Imagine what we can do with it against a team that doesn't even know we have the play!"

The smell of the rubbing alcohol was as sweet as perfume to Tim. The clouds of steam from the shower room were like a wonderful magic mist. He peeled off his practice jersey, happy to be alive. Things were certainly looking up for him. He had even blocked well most of the time that day. He was learning.

Tim hung his helmet on the hook in his locker and sat down on the wooden bench. He stretched his arms, feeling good all over. Everybody was happy. Coach Bronco was laughing and telling stories, and Tim walked over to join the crowd of players around him. The coach was telling the boys about a football dinner he had attended during the summer.

"It was a great night," Coach Bronco said. "All the

big stars were there. Sam Huff of the Giants, Jimmy Brown of the Cleveland Browns, Johnny Unitas of the Baltimore Colts. They all spoke to us and they made some fine speeches. Huff told a really funny story. Old Sam stood up there at the head table and pointed at Jimmy Brown. 'You see that guy Brown?' Huff said. 'Well let me tell you what he once did to ole Sam Huff.' "

Coach Bronco paused. The room was quiet now. All the players were crowded around, listening. "It seems that it happened in a big game between Cleveland and the Giants a couple of years ago," Coach Bronco said. "Huff decided that he was going to try to get Jimmy real angry and maybe, by getting him angry, cut down Jimmy's chances of playing a good game. So the first time Brown carried the ball, Huff ran in and tackled him hard. Sam sat on top of him and when the referee blew the whistle to end the play, Sam didn't get up right away. Instead he kept sitting on Jimmy until all the other players were up. Then Sam looked down and said, 'Jimmy, you stink.'

"Well a couple of plays later, Brown ran with the ball again and, wouldn't you know it, once more Huff banged him to the ground. The same thing happened. Sam sat on top of Jimmy and stayed there until the referee blew the whistle three times. Then Sam got up and Jimmy got up and Sam looked Jimmy square in the eyes. 'Jimmy,' Huff said. 'You stink.' Brown didn't say a word. He just looked at Huff and walked back into the Cleveland huddle.

"On the very next play, the way Huff tells the story,

54

Jimmy ran with the ball again. Only this time Sam couldn't get him. Sam ran in and got set to make the tackle, but Jimmy faked every which way and shot right by Sam. Huff made a dive for him but ended up flat on his face. Jimmy kept running and nobody could catch him. He ran right over the goal line for a touchdown. Then, as Sam told it, Jimmy dropped the ball and stood in the end zone, waiting for Huff to get up. When Huff got up, Jimmy called to him. 'Hey, Huff,' Jimmy hollered. 'How do I smell from here?'"

Tim almost doubled over laughing and so did the other players. Coach Bronco waved to them and walked out of the locker room. As he closed the door, the boys were all trying to talk at once.

The locker room was alive with noise and, as usual, Hawkins' voice was the loudest. Tim suddenly realized that Hawkins was talking about him.

"Hey guys," Hawkins said. "Did you see Tim today? Did you see him talking with Hans the Nut?"

Hawkins roared with laughter. A lot of the other players laughed loudly, too.

Tim felt like walking up to Hawkins and punching him in the nose. Instead, he ripped off his shoulder pads and threw them with a thump to the floor. Then he kicked off his shoes and let them fall hard on the concrete.

Tim wheeled around. "Look, you guys," he said. "Just because Hans is old and doesn't talk the way we do doesn't mean he is a nut. He is a smart man and he knows a lot. I enjoyed talking to him. I am going to keep on talking to him, too. And if any of you guys would try it, you would find out he is okay."

But Hawkins was not through. "You kidding, Boswell?" he said. "Everybody knows Hans is a nut. I guess old Hans got hit on the head too much for his own good when he played. Everybody knows he is crazy. And you know something else? If you enjoy talking to him so much you must be a nut, too."

Tim doubled his fists and took two steps toward Hawkins. Then he turned and walked back to his locker. He took off the rest of his uniform and stormed into the shower room. He turned on the cold water full blast and let it pour down, cooling him off, washing away his anger. There would be real trouble between them some day. Tim knew it and he knew that Len Hawkins knew it.

## chapter 5

# TIM LEARNS A LESSON

Coach Bronco was angry. He stood in front of the freshman football team for a full minute without speaking, staring straight ahead. Then he looked at each player, his eyes blazing.

"This is supposed to be a football team," he said. His voice was shaking with anger. His words echoed from end to end of the empty stadium. "This is supposed to be a football team, but it isn't even close. We have played three games and we have lost three games. Why? Is it because we don't know our plays?"

Coach Bronco stuffed his huge hands into his pockets. He answered his own question. "Of course, we know our plays," he said. "We know all our fancy plays. But they aren't working in the games. Why?"

He pulled his hands out of his pockets. Again he answered his own question. "Our plays aren't working," he said, "because the most fancy plays in the world will never work if the players don't know how to do the simple things first. And you fellows don't know how to do the simple things. You don't know how to tackle and you don't know how to block. To me, that means that you don't know how to play football. It is as simple as that. If you were blocking and tackling the way I have been teaching you to do, we would be winning our games."

Tim was sure the coach was staring straight at him, talking for his benefit.

"Well, we are going to learn the simple things," Coach Bronco boomed. "We are starting in right from the beginning. We are going to learn by practice—today and every day until we know our stuff. You fellows are going to be blocking and tackling in your sleep before I am finished."

Coach Bronco grabbed his whistle and held it high. "Not only are we going to go through all our old running and passing drills, we are going to start from the beginning." Coach Bronco stuffed the whistle in his mouth. He blew three blasts on it. "Let's get going," he yelled, "get the rubber tires out!"

Tim ran along beside Sammy Swift as the team headed toward the stands at the end of the field. There the players formed a line and hauled old rubber tires out of the shed that was under the stands. The tires were brought out on the field and placed side by side in two long rows, stretching from the 10-yard line to the 30-yard line. Tim and the others worked fast and seriously.

When the tires were set in place, the players began the drill, running through the rows of tires. Each player ran hard, his right foot pounding into the circle of a tire in one row, his left foot pounding into the circle of the tire in the other row. It was not an easy exercise but it would teach them to twist and dodge players while running with speed down the field.

Tim enjoyed the drill. It gave him a chance to turn on the speed and to dodge and twist the way he had always done when he had been playing fullback. He was good at the drill, too. It was difficult at first to get the right pace, but Tim quickly got his stride. He never once missed a step in all the times he ran back and forth through the rows of tires.

"Wind practice," Coach Bronco boomed. "Everybody ready for wind practice." The players pulled the tires off the field and put them back into the shed.

They lined up in three rows in the end zone. Tim, Hawkins, Chuck and Sammy Swift were in the front row. Coach Bronco stood at the edge of the field, giving the signals.

"Go!" the coach yelled.

The first row of players took off. They ran faster and faster toward the 50-yard line. Tim felt his lungs bursting as he tore across the field, kicking up dirt. Sammy Swift shot over the 50-yard line, with Tim and Hawkins right behind him. Chuck and almost all the others were a little farther back. Jack Gerard came in last, at least ten yards behind the others. Jack was puffing. "This kind of drill isn't for me," he said. "I like the 'rock-them-and-sock-them' of football, but I would just as soon leave the running to the rabbits."

No sooner were the words out of Jack's mouth when Coach Bronco's voice boomed again.

"Go!" the coach yelled, and the second row of players ran straight ahead from the end zone to the 50-yard line. "First row, get back here," Bronco said. "Get back here on the double."

The third row ran, then the first row ran again. Wind practice was tough. When they had reached the 50-yard line the second time, Tim tapped Jack on the shoulder. "Jack," he said. "You are so right. Running is definitely for rabbits."

But work was only beginning. Before he had come to State U., Tim had heard many stories about Coach Bronco. Tim had heard, of course, about what a great football player Bronco had been. But Tim had also heard how tough a coach Bronco could be. "When Bronco gets angry and decides he has to work his team hard," Tim had been told by one of the varsity players, "there is no coach who can be as tough."

Tim thought about that as he heard Coach Bronco

boom out the next orders. "Boswell and Hawkins," the coach said. "Get three tires from the shed and bring them over to the goal posts."

When they had brought the tires out, Coach Bronco took three chains out of the equipment bag. "Hang the tires from the cross-bar," he said. Jug jumped on Hawkins' shoulder. Tim gave Jug a tire and Jug fastened it to the far left side of the wooden cross-bar. Then Hawkins moved to the center of the cross-bar, and Tim handed up another tire. They put the third tire up at the far end of the cross-bar.

"All the backfield men get out to the 15-yard line," the coach said. "All you linemen get behind the tires, behind the end zone."

Tony Russo, the team manager, dumped a bag of footballs on the field. The backfield men lined up in three rows and began taking turns throwing the footballs toward the tires. The idea was to throw the ball through the hole. "Throw that ball through the hole often enough," Coach Bronco said, "and you will be able to pass the ball right into the arms of your team mate every time."

Tim and the other linemen chased the balls as they flew past the tires. Billy Wilson was the only lineman who wasn't chasing balls. He was with the backfield men, practicing his throwing for the end-around pass play.

After half an hour, the tires came down. Blocking and tackling practice began. Tim and the others rushed the dummies, blocking or tackling them. "Hit them low," he said to himself, over and over again. He rushed the dummies time and time again, always aiming low, always smacking straight into them.

Then the players began practice blocking against each other. The sweat was running down Tim's face. He ached all over. It was almost like the first week of practice. His shoulder pads felt heavy. His helmet weighed a ton. Each shoe felt anchored to the ground.

Tim wasn't doing so well in this drill. It was one thing to throw a clean, low block at a dummy, but quite another to try to hit a moving man. He kept moving in on his man, watching below the man's knees, his eyes always on the place he wanted to hit. But a quick movement by the player usually sent Tim's block too far to the side where it did no good in stopping the man.

Tim didn't know exactly what he was doing wrong. "I have to try harder," he said to himself. Tim gritted his teeth and dropped into a three-point position, lined up against Jack Gerard. Tim fastened his eyes below Jack's knees and rushed forward to block him. Jack stepped sharply to the left and Tim missed the block completely, falling flat.

Coach Bronco blew his whistle sharply. "Boswell, Boswell, Boswell," he yelled. "Where are your eyes when you start to block a man? Where are you looking?"

Tim rubbed the dirt off his face. "At his legs," he said. "I look below his knees, where I want to hit him."

Bronco banged his hands together. "No! No! No!" The coach blew his whistle. The other players had stopped practicing now, and were listening to Tim and the coach. "Everybody back to practice," he said. "Boswell, come here."

Tim ran to the coach. Coach Bronco began to speak slowly, carefully. His voice was low and firm. "Don't keep your eyes on a man's legs," he said. "Don't keep your eyes on his head or on his shoulders, either. Everybody fakes with his feet, head or shoulders, hoping to throw the man off balance. You faked with your feet and shoulders when you were a fullback. You fake with them now, right?"

"Right, Coach," Tim said.

"But no matter how much you fake, only your hips move in the direction in which you are really going. You watch your man's *hips*, not his legs, not his shoulders, not his head. You keep your eyes on his hips and you throw your body at his legs, low. Wherever his hips are, that is where he will be when he finally makes his move. Get in there now and try it."

Tim ran on to the field. He lined up against Billy, getting down low in his tackle's position. He kept his eyes on Billy's hips. Billy moved left, then right but Tim's eyes never left Billy's hips. As Billy dodged, Tim dived in low and dumped him to the ground, his shoulder catching Billy right between the ankles and the knees. It was a perfect low block.

"Good block," Billy said, as they scrambled to their feet. "You really dumped me hard."

Again and again, Tim lined up, watched his man's hips and pounded him to the ground with perfect low blocks. "Good blocking, Boswell," Coach Bronco said.

For almost an hour the players practiced. At long last, Coach Bronco blew his whistle. "Practice is over," he boomed. "Tomorrow we start all over again. This is one State U. team that is not going to lose any more games because of bad blocking and tackling."

Tim walked slowly to the locker room. Each step was an effort. He felt he couldn't have run if his life had depended on it.

When Tim walked into the locker room he was sure he had never smelled so much rubbing alcohol in his life. There was a long line of players standing at the rubbing table. Everybody wanted to have the aches and pains rubbed out. There was another long line at the whirling bath. Tim looked at it. "Boy," he thought, "would that feel good now." He decided to sit by his locker and wait until the bath line grew smaller. He thought of how good it would feel to sit in the round tub and let the warm water whirl around him, over his sore arms and legs.

Tim hung his helmet on the hook over his locker. He stripped off his shirt and shoulder pads and took off his shoes. His feet seemed to pop up to double their size when he took off the snug shoes. He sat down slowly on the bench and stretched his legs out in front of him. Chuck sat down next to him.

"How do you feel?" Tim asked.

"I never felt so tired in my life," Chuck said. "Every muscle in my body aches. How do you feel?"

"Tired, too," Tim said.

"Well, it's no wonder! We gave ourselves quite a workout today. What do you think of me as a slave driver?"

"Pretty rough, I must say." Tim grinned. "But inside I feel great. You know, Chuck, I think I am finally on my way to becoming a good tackle."

## chapter 6

# WORDS OF WISDOM

Tim ate quickly. As usual, steaks were piled high on the team's training table. Platters of green vegetables surrounded the steaks and large bowls of salad were set side by side in the middle.

When Jug offered him a second steak, Tim shook his head and said, "No, thanks."

"Hey," Chuck said, "you are slipping. You can usually eat three steaks. What's the matter? Sick?"

Tim smiled. "No, not sick," Tim said. "In a hurry. I have to be at Professor Billings' house in 15 minutes."

Hawkins took a bite of steak. "What do you know?" Hawkins said. His words were not clear because his mouth was full. "Teacher's pet."

Tim stared at him.

"Asking for extra help from teacher," Hawkins said. "Isn't that a good boy."

"Look, Hawkins," Tim said. "In the first place, Professor Billings asked me to come to his house. I didn't ask him if I could come. And in the second place, it is none of your business."

Jack Gerard leaped to his feet. "What is the matter with you two guys?" the stumpy guard said. "You haven't said two pleasant words to each other since we came to school. Come on, cut it out."

Tim put his hands on the edge of the table and pushed back his chair. He stood up and walked out of the dining room. Behind him, he heard Hawkins' voice. "Want an apple for the teacher?" Hawkins called. "We have apples here. Come on back and get one for teacher! You'd look just fine carrying one to teacher!"

Tim was worried that he had to go to see Professor Billings. He knew he was not doing too well in the professor's English class. "Maybe I am not working hard enough," Tim thought, as he walked under the trees across the college grounds.

Tim stared into the dark evening sky. He could not find a star and there was no moon. He had a strange feeling, walking along the lane, with only the yellow glare from the lamps to guide him. A shiver ran up his spine, and he began to walk faster.

As Tim neared the end of the lane he heard a noise

like that of wood being dragged along concrete. He slowed his pace and continued down the lane, around the curve. Suddenly, an overhead light went on and Tim jumped. He saw Hans, standing at the top of a step ladder. He had just replaced a burned-out bulb in the lamp. Tim laughed out loud when he realized what it was that had frightened him.

Tim walked up to the ladder. "Hello, Hans," he said.

"Hello, young man," Hans said. "How are you?"

"Pretty good," Tim said.

"How is your football?"

"Getting better," Tim said. "But now it is my studies that have me in trouble. I am on my way to Professor Billings' house right now. He wants to talk to me about my English."

"He is a good man, Professor Billings," Hans said. "You talk to Professor Billings and you listen," Hans said. "He knows a lot. He will help you."

Hans picked up the ladder and started to walk slowly up the lane. Before he had gotten far, he turned and said, "But he can help you only if you help yourself. Good night, young man."

Tim cut across the lawn behind the library, thinking of what Hans had said. "But he can help you only if you help yourself." Tim had heard that before, but he had never really taken the time to consider its meaning. "I guess it is like what happened to Willie Williams," Tim thought. "Sure, that must be it."

Tim would never forget Willie Williams. They had grown up together and, from the time they were seven years old, they had played ball together.

"Willie was sure to be a great football player," Tim thought, as he walked across the State U. campus. "He had everything."

Tim remembered what everyone had been saying when he and Willie were freshmen at Grand High. Why, Tim's own father had even said that, by the time Willie graduated, he would be one of the biggest high school football stars in the whole country.

But Willie's speed and natural skill were not enough. At Grand High, the football coach had spent hours working with Willie. "Williams," the coach had said, "you are the fastest runner on this team. But all your speed is going to waste because you don't know how to carry the football. Don't hold the football out in front of you when you run. If you hold it out, someone on the other team just has to slap at it and he can knock the ball right out of your hands. Tuck it into your stomach. If you will just learn that, nobody will be able to stop you. Let it become so natural that you won't have to waste a second of a game reminding yourself how to carry the ball. The way you are doing it now, you run for big gains every once in a while, but you fumble the ball, too."

"The coach keeps bugging me about holding the ball tight to my belly," Willie had said to Tim after the day's practice was over. "But it doesn't feel right there. Heck, I have gained enough for the team this season. I have the speed and, once I get free, no one can catch me. I just can't see that carrying the ball that way makes much difference."

"Willie just wouldn't listen," Tim thought. "The coach tried to help him, but Willie couldn't feel comfortable carrying the ball the way the coach wanted him to."

And then there was the day of the big game with Martin High. Willie had scored a touchdown right in the first quarter, but the kick for the extra point had been blocked. Grand High had played great defense, and they were still ahead, 6–0, in the middle of the fourth quarter. With just three minutes left to play in the game, Tim, Willie and the rest of the boys were feeling great.

"My touchdown is really standing up," Willie had said to Tim during a brief time-out period. "I don't think the coach will argue about the way I carried the ball. We have this game sewed up."

The referee blew his whistle ending the time-out period, and the players went into a huddle. The Grand High quarterback called for a running play. Willie was going to carry the ball. The team lined up and the ball was snapped back to the quarterback, who gave it to Willie. Willie took off, running as fast as he could, holding the ball out in front of him.

He dodged one Martin man, then another, cutting sharply toward the sidelines. Suddenly, a Martin player made a dive at him, hands flying. Willie dodged and the Martin man missed the tackle. But his right hand, Tim remembered, just managed to hit the ball.

The ball went flying from his hands into the air and, in a second, a Martin player was there, grabbing the ball. Before anyone knew what happened, he ran over the goal line for a touchdown. Martin kicked the extra point and Grand High lost, 7–6.

After that game, the coach had talked to Willie. It was not until two days later, when the players had gathered for practice, that they realized that Willie had been sent down to the second team.

The coach had done all he could to help Willie, but Willie had not wanted to help himself.


Tim arrived at Professor Billings' house and knocked on the door. A minute later, Professor Billings' thick body filled the entrance. He was fat and about five feet, seven inches in height. He smiled and pushed his glasses up from his nose. "Come in," he said. "Come in, Tim."

Professor Billings walked through a long hall, opened a door at the end of it and asked Tim into the room. "This is my study," he said. Tim stared at the books all around the room. "He must have a million books in here," Tim thought. The professor sat down behind a gleaming desk with a big globe on top of it. Tim sat in an armchair and waited for him to speak.

"Tim," the professor said. "You know you are not doing too well in my English Literature course. There is even a chance that you might not pass, if you don't improve."

Tim nodded silently. He had hoped it wouldn't be this bad.

"I wish you had come to me first," the professor said. "I want you to know one thing, I am here to teach you and help you. I have helped a lot of football players at State U. We have had several All-America football players here. Remember Wally Winston?"

Tim nodded. Who could forget Wally Winston, the great fullback?

"Well, Wally and I often talked," Professor Billings said. "We talked about studying and we talked about football, and nobody ever thought Wally was a sissy for coming to talk to me."

Tim almost laughed out loud. The idea of anyone calling Wally Winston a sissy struck him as funny.

"Tim," Professor Billings said, "what is your ambition? What do you want to be when you leave college?"

Tim did not hesitate even an instant before he gave his answer. "A professional football player."

"I thought so," the professor said. "Well, I want to show you how keeping up with your studies is necessary for your success in professional football. We can't just stuff information into you. Yes, I am sure you study hard, but I am afraid that you just read your books without thinking about what you are reading."

Tim stared at the professor. The glasses had slipped down again and they were resting at the tip of Professor Billings' nose.

"Almost every professional football player is a college graduate," the professor said. "You need a college education just to be able to understand the game. For instance, did you ever see a professional football player's book of plays?"

"No, sir," Tim said.

"Well, it is about 200 pages long, and the player has to know everything on every page. He has to know every one of the plays. He has to know why every one of the plays continue to be the best. He just can't *know* what each one is. He has to understand them. He has to think about them. Do you know that Raymond Berry of the Baltimore Colts spends at least three hours a night just *reviewing* his play book? He has to do it, and he is one of the biggest stars in the game. You can't let down even when you are on top.

"Professional football players spend hours watching films of their games, too. They watch films of other games. They have to watch every movement. They have to understand every play. Professional football is a combination of brains and muscle. You cannot succeed in it unless you have both. And, by learning to think in college, you will develop your brain power. No matter what you do later on in life, you have to improve your mind if you want to make a success out of life." The professor stopped talking and sat back in his chair.

Tim rubbed his hands together. He sat up straight in his chair and looked long at Professor Billings. "I never knew that so much brain work went into professional football," he said.

There was a knock then on the door of the study. Professor Billings got up. A tall, blonde girl was standing in the doorway. She was about five feet, eight inches tall, Tim guessed, and definitely pretty.

"Come in, Carol," Professor Billings said.

Professor Billings asked Carol to sit down. Then he turned to Tim. "Tim Boswell," he said, "this is Carol Roberts."

Tim stood up and, as he shook her hand, he said, "Hello, Carol."

"Glad to meet you," Carol said.

The professor reached down and took a large brown

envelope out of Carol's hand. "This is a special report that Carol has been doing for me," he said. "She came over to talk with me about it now. Let's see, what time is it? Seems early, Carol," he smiled at her.

Professor Billings pushed his glasses up from the point of his nose and looked at his wrist watch. "Eight o'clock," he said.

Tim moved toward the door. "Well, then," he said, "I guess I had better go."

"Wait just one second," Professor Billings said. "Remember what I was telling you a few minutes ago about brains and muscle? Well, Carol has the girls' combination of that. She has brains and beauty."

Tim saw Carol blush.

"Carol is one of the smartest girls in the freshman class," the professor said. "If you need any help studying, why don't you ask Carol some time?"

It was Tim's turn to blush. He looked down at the thick, blue carpet. "I would be happy to have her help," he said, "if it is okay with her."

Carol looked up and smiled. "It would be fine with me," she said. "We can study between halves of the football games," she joked. "I am a freshman cheer leader, so I see all the games."

Tim laughed. "I don't think Coach Bronco would like that too much," he said.

"Neither do I," Carol said. "But, seriously, any time you want some help, call me. I live at the freshman girls' dormitory."

Professor Billings opened the door of the study. "Thank you for coming over, Tim," he said. "I will let you find your own way out."

"Thank you, Professor. Nice meeting you, Carol. Good-by."

"Nice meeting you, Tim."

Tim walked through the hall and out the front door. He was smiling. "Carol Roberts," he said to himself. He stopped and pulled out his notebook and wrote down Carol's name.

He smiled again, happy with the world, and began to walk back toward his dormitory, whistling as loud as he could and, for once, in tune.

## chapter 7

# "HURRAH FOR HAWKINS"

Tim bounded down the dormitory steps, ran through the front hall, jumped over the railing on the porch, and landed on the wet grass in front of the building. His parents and his ten-year-old brother, Terry, were there waiting for him. Tim kissed his mother, shook hands with his father, and mussed Terry's hair. His family was at State U. to see him play in the game against the Abernathy College freshman team.

This was the first time Tim had seen his parents since school began and he wanted to tell them everything. He wanted to show them all the sights at once. They walked along the lanes, tall trees on either side, everybody talking at the same time. Tim heard all about his old high school friends.

Every once in a while as they walked, the wind would shake the trees and water would come sprinkling down.

Tim looked up at the sky, filled with black clouds. "Looks as if it may rain during the game," he said. "I bet the field will be soft and muddy. It will be a tough game, running in all that mud."

They walked on. Tim showed them the library and the chapel. He pointed to each of the buildings and told his parents what went on in them. "That is where I have my English class," he said, pointing to a big gray building that looked something like an old castle. "And that small building behind it is where I have my history class."

"Tim," his father asked, "how are you getting along in your classes?"

"Okay, I guess," Tim said. "I am having trouble in some but I am doing okay in most of them."

Mr. Boswell was almost as big as Tim. At the age of 44, Tim's father was still athletic. He played tennis and golf. People always said that sports skills ran in the Boswell family.

The Boswells made a complete circle around the campus and, when they reached Tim's dormitory again, Tim suggested they sit for a few minutes on the porch. Tim sat down on a bench between his mother and father.

Then Tim talked about his studies and told his father about the trouble he was having.

"You must not only read your books," Tim's father

said after Tim had finished. "You must understand them. Think about them. If you do that and come to understand what you are reading, it will help you in anything you ever want to do. This kind of thinking will help you in football, too. It will help you learn to be a good player at your new position."

"That is just what Professor Billings told me," Tim said, surprised.

Tim's mother wanted to know if Tim was getting enough to eat. She wanted to know if he needed anything from home, if his room was comfortable, not too hot, not too cold. She wanted to know all about his friends. Tim told her that everything was fine. He said it was great having his friend, Chuck, as his room mate, and he told about Billy Wilson and Cliff Zanger, and Jack Gerard and Sammy Swift. But he did not tell her about Len Hawkins.

Suddenly, a sprinkling rain began to fall. Tim looked at his wrist watch. It was almost 12 o'clock. "We had better get going," he said. "I have to be at the football field in 15 minutes. We are playing in the big stadium today since the varsity team is playing out of town."

"Aren't you going to eat lunch?" Tim's mother asked.

Tim smiled. "No, Mom," he said. "We eat a big breakfast, steak and eggs and everything, on the day of a game and don't eat again until supper."

Terry now came running around from behind the bench. Tim's mother told Terry to put on his raincoat.

"It is not raining hard," he said. Before he could say another word, Tim threw the rubber yellow raincoat at him, and laughed. "Same old Terry," he laughed. "Put on the raincoat, boy, before I get tough."

Terry put on the raincoat, and, as Tim said good-by to him and his parents, Terry yelled, "Today is the day you get a touchdown, Tim! Get a touchdown for me!"

Tim's smile faded and a frown creased his face. "I don't score touchdowns any more, Terry," he said. "I am not a fullback any more. I play tackle. I told you that before. I am a tackle now."

Terry looked up at Tim. "You can still score a touchdown," he said. "I want to hear them cheering for you. Then I can cheer with them, as I did last year. Boswell, Boswell, rah-rah-rah." Terry leaped into the air and clapped his hands.

Tim said nothing. Instead, he looked again at his watch. "I really have to go now. See you later." He forced a smile, and started toward the football field. As he walked, he shook his head as though to shake off a feeling of sadness. "They don't cheer for me any more," he said to himself. "They cheer for the men who score the touchdowns. Okay, so what, Tim Boswell? You have your job. Go do it."

Tim hardly heard Coach Bronco's pep talk, and he ran through the exercises and drills as if he were in a dream. The rain had begun to come down hard. It was pounding the field as the game began, soaking the grass, turning the dirt into mud. The people in the stands sat close together under umbrellas, and wrapped in raincoats. The boys on the bench had on big coats with hoods over their heads. The cheer leaders' cards, which had State U. printed on them in bright green letters, were dripping wet.

Tim's white uniform became smeared with mud almost as soon as the game started. State U. elected not to pass the ball. It was too wet for pass plays, even though the ball was thrown over to the side of the field after every play and dried with towels. Cliff would bend over the ball at center and try to protect it from the rain with his body, and Chuck would dry his hands on the towel tucked under Cliff's belt in the back, but still, by the time the play began, the ball was always too wet for Chuck to throw well.

Tim slipped around in the line. On one play he and Jack slid right into each other. Abernathy College was having the same trouble. The Abernathy freshmen couldn't work any pass plays, either, but in the second quarter, they worked a beautiful running play. Somehow their quarterback managed to hide the ball as he faked handing it to the halfback. All the State U. line tackled the halfback and the Abernathy quarterback ran 40 yards through the mud to score a touchdown.

At halftime, the State U. team trooped unhappily to the locker room. They were losing, 6–0, and it didn't look as if they would ever score. Their faces and uniforms were caked with mud. Tim took off his helmet and dropped it on the bench in front of him. Tony Russo, the team manager, was walking alongside the benches, passing out towels to the players. Tim took a towel and wiped the mud from his face. Then he took off his cleats and banged them together, knocking the mud from the bottom of the shoes.

Russo walked down between the benches, carrying a tray of sliced oranges. The players reached in and helped themselves. Tim took two of the slices, and put one in his mouth. The orange tasted good, and pepped him up a little.

Russo walked back with the empty tray, collecting the orange peels. Tim dropped his peels on the tray, and leaned back and stared at the ceiling. He was twice as tired as he usually was at halftime. He realized that playing in mud took a lot of energy.

Coach Bronco walked into the locker room. The rain was dripping off his hat, which he threw on a hook before taking off his soaked raincoat. He stood in front of the benches, his hands digging down into the pockets of his blue pants. He stared up and down the rows of players, then began to speak softly.

"I know what you are all thinking," Coach Bronco said. "You are all thinking how terrible it is that the field is muddy and that you can't get any of your plays working. You are all thinking that if the weather were nice you could go out and beat the blazes out of this team."

Some of the players began to nod, agreeing with the coach. Suddenly, Coach Bronco's voice boomed.

"Well, stop thinking that right now," he bellowed. "And don't ever think about anything like that as long as you play football at State U. So the mud is messing up our plays. Well, what do you think the mud is doing to the Abernathy plays? It is doing the same thing, that's what. Both teams are playing in the mud. But one team is losing. We are losing. Why are we losing? I say we are losing because we are too interested in thinking about how the mud is messing up our plays."

Tim leaned forward on the bench. He looked down at the floor and stared at the streaks of mud that the players had tracked in. Coach Bronco was quiet for a second, then he continued.

"Well, from this moment on, we are going to play football," the coach said. "You know how you win a football game in the mud? You win it by playing harder than you play at any other time. You win it by playing as hard as you can and by thinking about the two most important things—your blocking and tackling. The team that blocks the hardest and tackles the hardest wins games in the mud. You can't use any passing plays. You have to run with the ball, and you won't gain a yard in this mud unless the blocking is good and hard. And you can't stop the other team unless the tackling is hard. I want to see you get out there in the second half and trounce those guys. I want to *hear* those blocks. I want to *hear* those tackles. Right now I am disgusted with you. I don't even want to stay in this room with you."

Coach Bronco grabbed his hat and shoved it on his head. Drops of water came sprinkling down from the hat. He threw on his raincoat and stomped out of the locker room.

Tim pulled on his cleats. He leaped up and grabbed his helmet. "Let's get out there and get them," he yelled.

"Right," Jack yelled. "This half we get them."

The State U. freshman football players ran out the door, roaring at the top of their lungs. They were shouting and cheering as they came out on the field.

'During the second half, Tim blocked hard and tackled well. Chuck called all the State U. trick running plays, but none of them worked in the slippery mud.

All too soon it was late in the fourth quarter. State U. was still behind, 6–0. Now State had the ball on its own 15-yard line. Chuck called for an end run play. Sammy Swift came running from his halfback position, and Chuck handed him the ball. Sammy started to run around end but the wet ball squirted out of his hands. It was a fumble!

Tim and Hawkins made a dive for the bouncing ball, but the Abernathy right end got there first and fell on the football. State U. had lost the ball!

Three times, Abernathy tried to crack through the center of the State U. line, and all three times Tim, Jack

and Cliff managed to stop them. It was fourth down.

Tim dug in hard, ready to crack through the Abernathy line. He looked up and saw that Abernathy was getting ready for a field goal. The stand was rocking with noise. "Block that kick! Block that kick!"

The cheers continued to roll down. Hands were clapping and people were yelling: "State U.! State U.! Fight, fight, fight!"

The Abernathy center snapped the ball. Their quarterback grabbed it and placed it on the kicking tee. Tim came roaring through the line, Jack and Billy tearing through with him. The Abernathy kicker smashed his foot into the ball. Tim rose with the kick and the ball hit with a thud against his chest. The ball was smothered by Tim, Jack and Billy.

The State U. fans went wild. "Blocked kick! Blocked kick!" They were waving wet pennants. State U. still had a chance. There was one minute left in the game—still time to score one touchdown. A touchdown would tie the game. A good kick after the touchdown would win it!

Chuck called a pass. "Keep the ball as dry as you can," he pleaded to Cliff. State lined up. Tim took a solid stand. The ball was snapped and Chuck faded back. Now he had to throw fast while the ball and his hands were still dry. He ran back away from State U.'s 20-yard line.

Tim rushed forward watching the opposing man's hips. He hit his man hard and low, pounding him to the ground. Tim looked up and saw the football flying down the field. He saw Billy leap into the air and grab the ball. A great pass. A great catch. State U. had gained forty yards. The ball was on the Abernathy 40-yard line.

The stands rocked with noise! "State U.! State U.! Rah-rah-rah!"

Chuck called another pass play. Again he faded back, bent his arm, waited for his man, and threw perfectly. With a thump, the ball landed smack in Billy's stomach. Now the ball was on the Abernathy 10-yard line, and there were ten seconds left in the game. Time for one more play.

Chuck yelled, "Three back down play." It was the play

in which the fullback smashed up the middle. "Line up," Chuck yelled. "Line up."

Cliff bent over the ball. Chuck lined up behind him. Tim and Jack dug in. They had to open up a hole for Hawkins to run through.

Chuck barked out the signals. He grabbed the ball and shoved it into Hawkins' hand, as the big fullback cracked forward. Tim and Jack pushed two players out of the way, opening up a hole for Hawkins. Hawkins came charging through, his shoes slipping in the mud, but the big fullback wasn't stopping. He banged ahead, step by step, toward the goal line. He was over. He was in the end zone. It was a touchdown! State U. had tied the score.

Cheers rolled down with a roar from the stands. Then the stands grew quiet. State U. still had to kick the extra point to win. It was up to Hawkins. He was the State U. place kicker.

Cliff snapped the ball straight back to Chuck, who planted it firmly on the kicking tee. Tim blocked as if his life depended on it.

Hawkins approached the ball. He kicked it hard and high, up over the goal posts. It was a good kick! It was an extra point! State U. had won the game, 7–6!

The State U. players pounded each other on the back. Coach Bronco was smiling, his face lighted up with a great big grin. Tim ran through the rain to the locker room. He was happy now for his team had won the game and he had played well. He hadn't missed a single block all during the game. He had tackled hard, and he had blocked a kick, besides.

Behind him, Tim heard the cheers from the stands. They were loud, wild cheers, the happy cheers of victory. Hands were clapping and voices were singing and yelling.

"Hurrah for Hawkins! Hurrah for Hawkins!"

"Haw-kins! Haw-kins! Rah-rah-rah."

Tim stopped short as he ran into the locker room. Above all the noise, he could hear Hawkins' booming voice. "It is what I have been telling you guys all along," Hawkins said. He saw Tim and stared at him. "Just block for me and I will score all the touchdowns you need."

## chapter 8

# TIM'S TROUBLES PILE UP

The State U. football field was alive with noise. Coach Bronco's booming commands were ringing in Tim's ears. "Leap in the air! Legs apart! Legs together! Fall on your face! Push up! Back on your feet!"

Tim was in the air, on the ground, leaping, straining, working hard, doing team exercises. His muscles were moving in time with the coach's commands. Tim didn't miss a beat. "If only I knew my plays as well," Tim thought.

A lot had happened in the two weeks since State U. had defeated Abernathy. The team had played two games. They had won the first and lost the second. Tim had been responsible for the loss. He had been caught out of position on a red dog play and the opposing halfback had run right through the big space Tim had left open.

Now the State U. freshman team's record was two wins and four losses. The team had lost two games because of Tim—the very first game when Tim hadn't blocked his man low and the latest game when Tim missed his man in the red dog play. The game had been played the day before and Coach Bronco had not said one word to Tim since.

Coach Bronco now put the whistle to his mouth and blew three sharp blasts. The players lined up in front of Coach Bronco.

"We are going to work on defense today," the coach said. "I am splitting up the first team. I want the first team backfield on offense and the first team line on defense. Let's go!"

Chuck, Hawkins, Sammy, and Jug ran out and lined up on offense. The second team line went with them. Tim, Jack, Billy, Cliff and the other boys from the first team line ran out on defense. The second team backfield was on their side for this practice.

The practice game began. Tim charged forward on the very first play and smashed Hawkins flat on his back. "Good tackle," Billy yelled. "Good tackle."

Hawkins got up and glared at Tim.

Tim stood at the line waiting for the next play to begin. The team on offense came running out. Tim set himself at tackle. Behind him, he heard Cliff call for red dog right.

"I cover up for him," Tim said to himself. "This time I will do it right."

The center snapped the ball. Cliff came charging past Tim and Tim dropped back to cover Cliff's position. Chuck had the ball and faked a pass. It was a beautiful fake. Tim was sure that Chuck was throwing the ball over the center of the line. Tim ran over to the man he thought Chuck was throwing the ball to but Chuck had not thrown it. Instead, he ran with the ball. He ran right through the spot Tim had left uncovered. He ran for twenty yards before he was finally tackled.

Coach Bronco blew his whistle. "Boswell," he boomed. "Get out of the game. Jennings, get in there in place of Boswell."

Tim walked slowly toward Coach Bronco, as the coach blew the whistle again.

"Get on with practice," he said to the players on the field.

Tim stood still and straight in front of the coach. "Boswell," Coach Bronco said. "I want you to go into the locker room and take a shower. I want you to get out of here and spend the rest of this afternoon thinking. Think about the red dog play until you know what it is all about. When you have thought so much about it that there is no more chance of your doing it wrong, come tell me. Right now, just get out of here."

Tim walked slowly toward the locker room. He stooped down and plucked a blade of grass. Inside he peeled off his uniform and stood for a long time under the shower. Outside, he could hear the thump of the crashing football players. He could hear their shouts. He was as downhearted as he had ever been in his life.

Tim began to think about the red dog play. Again and again he ran through it. He knew it by heart. But where was he making his mistake? "This is what Hans was saying about Professor Billings being able to help me only if I would help myself. Well, Coach Bronco has told me about the red dog play and now it is up to me. I only hope he gives me another chance."

Tim walked out of the shower room, dried himself and dressed. Then he went outside and walked, thinking about football, about the mistakes he was making, and about the red dog play. He couldn't help thinking, too, that all this trouble could have been avoided. "If I had stayed at fullback," he thought, "I would be scoring touchdowns and nobody would be bawling me out."

Tim wanted to talk to somebody. He had thought enough and now he wanted to be with someone. He decided to look for Hans. Tim walked around the college grounds but when he couldn't find the grounds keeper, he went back to his dormitory.

Inside the front hall, Tim had a thought. "I will call Professor Billings," he said to himself, "and go talk with him for a while." Tim went to the telephone booth and reached inside his pocket for a dime. Then he sat down in the booth, and dropped the coin in the slot and tried Professor Billings' number. The professor's housekeeper answered the phone and told Tim that the professor was not at home. "He is almost never at home on Saturday," she added.

Tim walked out into the front hall. He had forgotten it was Saturday because the freshman team had played yesterday, Friday. It had been the only time they had not played on a Saturday all season. "I am so mixed up," Tim told himself, "I even have the days mixed up."

He looked at his wrist watch. It was five o'clock. "Gee, that Latin-American music show is on now," he thought. "I will go up and tune in and take it easy for a little while."

Tim went upstairs and switched on the radio that he and Chuck kept on the dresser. The music poured out. It was thumping Latin music. Tim liked to dance to a good band. He had danced well in high school, but there hadn't been a chance to dance this fall in college. In fact, he hadn't had a single date since he had come to State U.

Tim slid through some dance steps. He thought about football, too. It was a funny thing that, because of football, Tim had become interested in dancing. Back in high school he had read a story about Jimmy Brown, the great fullback of the Cleveland Browns. The story said that Jimmy was excellent on the dance floor. It told how, before each Cleveland Brown football game, Jimmy Brown turned on the radio and danced—to relax his nerves and loosen his muscles.

It was no wonder that Tim had begun to like dancing after that. Tim wanted to do everything Jimmy did. After all, Jimmy Brown was the greatest fullback in professional football and Tim was a fullback, too, at that time.

"I am not a fullback any more," Tim thought, as he slid back and forth across the carpet, dancing to the music. "But I still like dancing."

Tim followed the music for almost half an hour. Then he lay down on his bed, pulled his loose leaf notebook from the shelf above and began to draw diagrams in it. He drew the red dog play, neat x's and o's, the way the coach always drew them when he was putting a play on the black board. The x's were the players on defense, the o's were the players on offense.

When Tim had drawn out the red dog play, he thought

about it. He was sure he could play it right. Another time he would not foul it up. "And if I do," he said to himself, "it won't be because I don't understand it. A red dog play is a surprise play. It throws the other team off balance. If I am at tackle, the man who is supposed to block me is lined up almost directly in front of me. He comes at me as soon as the play starts. But when I run back on the red dog play and he starts chasing me, then he leaves a hole open for the line backer to come through. And the line backer can get in to make a tackle. What I have to do is to block the line backer and make sure that I get back to the fellow with the ball, if he runs to the spot the line backer leaves open."

Tim had thought about that many times before. Coach Bronco had explained it to him. Maybe now, finally, it would work out.

Tim sat down at the desk and pulled a sheet of paper from the top drawer. It had been almost three days since he had written a letter home. He began to write and tried to make his letter seem as cheerful as possible. He wrote that things were pretty good with his football, and that his studies were going well. In fact, his studies were still not going at all well. And he suddenly realized that he had important tests coming up on Monday. "How did I ever forget them?" he thought. "Boy, am I mixed up today!"

He finished the letter quickly and went out into the hall to mail it. When he got back to his room, he hauled his English Literature book off the shelf over his bed.

He sat down at the desk and stared out the window. The sky was growing dark. The trees were moving slightly in the wind. Almost all the leaves had fallen off.

He brought his attention back to the book before him. "The biggest test of the term in the subject I am doing worst in, and I can't seem to get myself to think about it."

Tim's eyes were fastened on the book cover. He ran his hand over the book. He twisted in his chair and stood up. He walked over to the closet and opened it. A pile of clothes was right up front. "I have to get to the laundry soon," he thought, "or I won't have anything to wear."

Tim closed the closet door and walked back to his desk. He touched the cover of the book again and looked up toward the shelf over his bed. He stared at the latest football magazine on his shelf, but he knew he shouldn't read it. "I have to study," he said to himself. "I have to study."

Tim opened the English book and began to read. The words all came together; they didn't make sense. He stared at the pages and tried to remember what he had read, but he couldn't understand the words.

Suddenly, Tim was out of the chair. He reached up and pulled the football magazine from the shelf and fell back on his bed and began to read. There was a story in the magazine about the State U. varsity team. Tim had always dreamed about seeing his name in one of the big football magazines. "Maybe next year," he said to himself. "If I can get on the State U. varsity, maybe the magazine will write about me, too."

He stared out the window. Here he was thinking about playing for the State U. varsity and he wasn't even sure he would be in the starting line-up of the State U. freshman team. He slapped the magazine shut and tossed it back on the shelf. Then he went back to his desk and began to study again. Again the words just seemed jumbled. He read them over and over again. But he couldn't understand them.

Tim stood up and took off his tie and shirt. He walked to the sink and splashed some water on his face. Then he went past the desk and pulled down the football magazine again. He thumbed through the pages and spotted a story about one of his all-time favorite players, Sammy Baugh, the great passer who played for the Washington Redskins years ago.

Tim began to read the story. Halfway through it he came across something he had never read before. It was about Sammy Baugh when he first reported to the Washington Redskins, trying out for the professional team.

"In the first blackboard drill Sammy ever had with Washington coach Ray Flaherty," Tim read, "a play was outlined with *x*'s and *o*'s. Flaherty was talking as he put the play on the board, explaining it to Sammy. 'And when your receiver reaches this point,' Flaherty said, scratching out the point with the chalk, 'I want you to hit him in the eye with that pass.' Sammy looked up seriously, and said, 'Which eye?'"

Tim laughed. "Boy, what confidence," he thought.

Tim finished the story. He leaped up from the bed, walked over to the desk and picked up the book again and began reading. But he still couldn't keep his mind on the subject.

The door from the hall opened with a bang. Chuck came dashing into the room. "How are you?" Chuck said. "What a bad deal you got today! The coach didn't have to send you off the field. He should have worked with you."

"That is okay," Tim said. "I did what he said I should do. I thought about the red dog play. I really know it now."

Chuck's face was creased with a frown. His arms hung at his side. "I don't know," Chuck said. "Boy, I don't think I could be as calm as you are if the coach did that to me."

Tim smiled. "Chuck," he said, holding up his English Literature book, "if you think I have troubles in football, they are nothing compared to the real troubles I have. If I don't pass that English Literature test on Monday, I may not even be a student at State U., much less a tackle on their freshman team."

## chapter 9

# WHEN STUDY MAKES SENSE

Tim tried to study, but nothing he read seemed to make sense. He had to get help quickly. Tim took two steps toward the telephone booth and stopped. Then he took two steps away.

"Should I call Carol?" he asked himself. "She said she would help me study. I sure need somebody's help." He stopped again. "She will probably be out on a date. I should have called her before this."

He drew a deep breath and walked quickly to the telephone. He twisted his big body into the small booth and tried the number of the freshman girls' dormitory. He asked for Carol and soon he heard her voice.

He couldn't say a word at first, but, finally, he managed to speak.

"Hello," he said. "Is this Carol?"

"Yes."

"This is Tim Boswell. Tim Boswell, the football player. I mean, Tim Boswell, the fellow you met at Professor Billings' house."

"Yes, Tim," Carol said. "How are you?"

"Fine, how are you?" Then the words poured out. "If you are free tonight, could you help me study? I mean, you said if I called you, you might and I certainly can use some help. If you are not busy, I mean."

"Well, Tim, some of the other cheer leaders and I were going to work on some signs tonight, but I am sure they won't mind if I don't work with them. I will make it up with extra time during the week. So I would be glad to help you if I can. Why don't we meet in the library study hall in half an hour? Is that all right?"

"Fine! Great! I will be there on the button. Thanks. Thanks a lot."

"Good-by, Tim."

"Good-by."

Tim slapped the phone toward the hook. He missed. The phone slammed against the side of the booth and swung on its cord. He grabbed it and slammed it down on the hook. He ran out of the booth, up the dormitory steps and into his room.

Chuck swung around from the desk. "Where are you heading?" Chuck said.

"To study," Tim said.

"In such a hurry?"

"With Carol," Tim said.

"Oh, then I don't blame you." Chuck laughed.

Tim straightened his shirt and tie, smoothed his sports jacket, and went to the door. He bounded down the stairs, and went walking fast into the night, whistling.

Half the way up the lane toward the library, Tim suddenly stopped. He had been watching two people at the end of the lane from the time he had begun his walk. Now as he drew closer he could see who they were. One towered over the other. It was Hawkins, and he was with Hans.

"If that Hawkins is picking on Hans," Tim said to himself, "I am going to teach him a lesson he will never forget."

103

Tim doubled up his hands and left the path. He walked along behind the trees, being careful not to step on any branches. He weaved his way along until he was only five feet away from Hawkins and Hans. He stood out of sight, listening and watching.

Hans was looking up into Hawkins' eyes. The big full-back was talking. "You should be glad I walked by when I did. How did you fall into that ditch anyway?"

"I am so used to walking around here," Hans said, "that I wasn't looking. I have been here so long I think I know all the ground, but all of a sudden there is a ditch and I am in it."

Tim looked across the path, to a deep ditch, dug only the day before by men who were putting in a new pipe line for gas.

"Well, as long as you are not hurt, I will run along."

"All right, young man," Hans said. "And thank you again for helping me."

"Hawkins has never done anything to Hans but make fun of him." Tim thought. "It is strange that he should be the one to come by when Hans needed help. And why didn't he make fun of Hans the way he does behind his back?" Tim thought, as he waited quietly until Hans and Len Hawkins were out of sight before he continued on to the library.

Inside the building, Tim went quickly to the study hall. Carol was there waiting for him. Her blonde hair was shining in the light from the ceiling. "She looks prettier tonight than when I first saw her," Tim thought.

He stumbled over a chair as he wound his way among the tables toward Carol. "I am sorry to be late," he said.

Carol's face lit with a smile. "That's okay," she said. "I think I was a little early anyway."

Tim dropped his books on the table and flopped into the wooden chair next to Carol. "What a day!" he whispered. "I couldn't do a thing right."

"Still thinking about yesterday's game?" she said.

"How can I forget it? I lost the game for us."

"Lots of players have lost games," Carol said. "Cheer up. I just know you will make it up the next game."

Tim leaned back in his chair. It felt good to find someone who had confidence in him. Carol's voice was soft and pleasant and he began to feel happier.

Tim stared at the ceiling. Then he looked down at the books. "I don't know if I will ever help State U. win any games," he said. "I was telling my room mate, Chuck, tonight that if I don't pass that English Literature test on Monday, I may not even be here studying, much less playing football. Unless I keep up passing grades in every subject, no more money from the football fund will be given toward my college education, and my parents can't afford to pay all my way."

Carol's blue eyes sparkled. "Stop worrying," she said. "That is why I am here, to help you pass that test."

"I don't know," Tim said. "I have been reading Shakespeare over and over again. I can't seem to drum it into

my head. I read it and I think I understand it and then, on the tests, I don't know what is meant at all."

"Look, Tim," Carol said. "Anybody can work hard enough and long enough to learn almost anything by heart. But you forget it just as fast. The trick is to understand what you are reading while you are reading it. If it makes sense to you, then you won't have such trouble on your tests."

Carol reached over and picked up Tim's book. "Let me see if I can find an example that will help you see what I mean." She turned the pages of the book. "Here is a line from Shakespeare's play, *Twelfth Night*. Listen to what he wrote: 'Be not afraid of greatness: some are born great, some achieve greatness, and some have greatness thrust upon them.' Do you understand that?"

"I am not sure. Let's see how you would help me to understand it better."

"All right. Can you think of anybody who was born great?"

Tim thought for a while. "You know," he said, "I just can't see how anybody is *born* great."

"Well, how about George Washington?" Carol said.

Tim was quiet for a minute. "Oh, now I think I see what you mean," Tim said. "When you consider all Washington did during his life, it would seem that each thing he did was just one more step forward to his becoming the father of our country. Yes, I think Washington was born great."

"Good," Carol said. "Now can you name someone who achieved greatness?"

"You mean someone who had to work hard and teach himself?"

Carol nodded.

"Would a football player do?" Tim asked.

"Name one," Carol said, smiling.

"Raymond Berry of the Baltimore Colts," Tim said, remembering the player Professor Billings had talked about. "Ray was picked way down on the draft list by the Colts. Nobody thought he had a chance to make good in professional football. But he practiced long and hard, and he studied his plays and did whatever else he could to improve his playing so that, through his efforts, he made good and became an all-star end.

"Say, come to think of it, Carol, what made you want to become a football cheer leader?"

"I love sports. I have been a sports fan all my life," Carol said. "I almost had to be. My father played football in college and my two brothers played football and baseball in college. I learned everything from them.

"Now," Carol said, "back to work. Can you think of any person who had greatness thrust upon him?"

Tim thought for a minute, and then said, "How about former President Truman?"

"That's good," Carol said, "but why did you choose him?"

"Well, when President Roosevelt died in 1945, Vice President Truman overnight became President of the United States. He became the President of the United States at a very important time. He had to take charge of finishing up World War II and helping to start the United Nations. And because he did so well, he became great. He had greatness thrust upon him."

"That's the idea," Carol said. "You see what I mean. Just make yourself take the time to think about what you are learning. It takes more time and you might not always be successful, but before long you will score much better on your tests."

"I see," Tim said. "And you know something, I like it. When I start to think about Shakespeare like that it means something."

Tim's eyes sparkled as he and Carol continued with

his studies. Twice he had to be told to keep his voice down. The third time, Tim and Carol were told that it was closing time. Tim hadn't realized it was so late. He was smiling as he walked out of the library to take Carol back to her dormitory.

They walked along, talking about football and history and dancing and Shakespeare. "How about a date to celebrate?" Tim asked. "For Tuesday night. We will go out and celebrate my passing grades in history and English. I wish I could learn my football as easily."

"Don't let up, though," Carol said. "Keep on reading and think about what you are reading as we have tonight. You will soon find you are really learning."

"Who knows?" Tim said, laughing, "If I get a B, I may find I am having greatness thrust upon me!"

## chapter 10

# BOSWELL BATTLES BACK

Professor Billings stood in front of his freshman English Literature class.

"I have the results of the tests you took yesterday," he said. "They will be posted on the bulletin board this afternoon."

The professor pushed his glasses up from the tip of his nose. He smiled. "Most of you did very well." Suddenly his smile turned into a frown. "But some of you, I am afraid, failed."

Professor Billings paused. "That is all for today," he said. "Class is dismissed."

Tim stood up. He picked up his books and walked toward the door. "Tim," the professor called, "I would like to talk with you."

The rest of the class filed out of the room. Tim was alone with the professor. "I didn't pass the test," Tim said to himself. "That is what he wants to talk to me about. I thought I did well, but I guess I didn't."

Professor Billings was behind his desk. "Sit down, Tim," he said. Tim slipped into a wooden chair. He tapped his fingers against his notebook. "Tell me," Tim thought. "Get it over with. Don't make me wait."

Professor Billings smiled. "Tim," he said, "I am proud of you. You turned in an excellent test paper."

Tim drew a deep breath. His face grew into a great big smile. He wanted to laugh. It was wonderful.

"Take it easy," Professor Billings said. "I just wanted to chat with you. Tell me, Tim, how is your football?"

Tim's eyes grew troubled. A moment ago he had been so happy that he had almost forgotten that Coach Bronco had taken him off the first team. He had almost forgotten about Monday's practice when Coach Bronco had told him that from now on he would be playing with the second team.

"What do you think is wrong, Tim?"

"Oh, I don't know. I never was a tackle before. That is the reason, I guess. I was a fullback in high school. Now I have to learn a new position. Maybe there is too much for me to learn."

"Tell me, Tim," he said, "are you happy with your new position? Have you been happy with it from the beginning?"

"Honestly, I guess not. I liked it much better playing fullback."

"What do you miss most about not playing fullback? Tell me honestly, Tim."

"The truth? The truth is, I think I miss the cheers. I used to be a star. I used to get the glory."

"And now all you get is work, right?"

"Right. That's just the way my room mate and I put it. I get the work. Guys like Hawkins get the glory."

"That is what I thought, Tim," he said. "I think you are too concerned with that fact to do your best. Oh, I am sure you try hard but, in the back of your mind, you are thinking about Hawkins always running with the ball."

Tim tapped his notebook.

"Tim," Professor Billings said. "Do you remember Don Holleder, the fellow who played for Army maybe six or seven years ago?"

"No, I don't think so," Tim said.

"Well, let me tell you about Don. In his junior year at Army, Don was a great end, and everybody said that the next year Don would be the best end in college football. He even had an excellent chance of being the top football player in the whole country.

"But that next year, Army needed a quarterback, and Coach Blaik told Don to play quarterback because that was where the team needed him.

"At first, Don felt low. He said it was like starting

all over. He couldn't sleep and he kept wondering, 'Why me?'

"But then he got to thinking. If Coach Blaik thought he was the man to do the job, he should be flattered. One thing Don learned at West Point is that you get the job done. He would give it all he had, just as long as he was helping the team. Don played without complaint, giving up all his chances to become an All-America. He became a good quarterback, too. Not a great quarterback, but a good one. And he helped Army win games, losing his chance to gain personal glory."

Tim stared straight at the professor. His fingers were still. The notebook rested in his lap.

"Your case is a little different," Professor Billings said. "In fact, Tim, it is a lot different. Don Holleder was a senior. He knew he could never become a great quarterback in the one year he had left in college. But you are only a freshman, Tim. You can become a great tackle. You want to play professional football. Well, professional football teams need tackles. The tackles don't get the glory. All the other players know it and respect them for it. The players and the coaches know that they can't win games unless the tackles and the guards do their work well.

"Knute Rockne, the great coach at Notre Dame, once had a wonderful backfield called 'The Four Horsemen.' The Four Horsemen got all the glory and one day, Knute took his first team tackles, guards and center out of a game. He let the Four Horsemen play behind a second string line. The Four Horsemen could not gain a yard. 'I just wanted to prove that you boys won't get a bit of glory unless the linemen are in there with you, doing the heavy work,' Knute told them.

"A team knows that its success depends upon the boys in the line, Tim. You should be proud. Your team can't win unless you are doing your job. You should want to do your job better than anyone on the field. Remember that, work extra hard and forget about the glory. Then I am sure you will be a fine tackle.

"That is all I wanted to say, Tim."

"Thank you, Professor," Tim said.

Tim was out of the chair and out the door in a flash. He would try. After all, he had tried in English and he had passed the test. Well, he was going to pass his football test, too. If an All-America like Don Holleder could give up his big chance, so could a freshman player like Tim Boswell. Tim was going to play tackle some day in professional football. He was sure of that now. He would be the best tackle anybody had ever seen.

Tim couldn't wait for practice to start. At long last, his classes were over, and he was in the locker room. He grabbed his green practice jersey. He slapped on his shoulder pads and slipped the jersey over them. He dressed as fast as he had ever dressed in his life. He stopped only once. "Chuck," he yelled. "I passed the English test. I passed it with flying colors, Professor Billings said."

Tim was out on the field before anyone else. He was all set to go. Nobody was going to stop him. He was going to line up with that second team and whack away at that first team so hard they wouldn't know what hit them. He whipped through the exercises. He ran around the field. He was ready.

Finally, Coach Bronco blew the whistle. Tim was in his position before the coach even finished reading off the second team line. "Boswell, tackle," he boomed, and Tim was out there. The others lined up around him.

The first team had the ball. Cliff Zanger bent over it at center. Chuck stood behind him. Tim was lined up at defensive tackle, ready to crash between Jack Gerard and Ronnie Updike, the boy who had taken his place on the first team. Cliff snapped the ball and Tim went blasting into the backfield. Updike never had a chance to stop him. Tim bowled Updike over and tore after Chuck.

Chuck faded back to pass, Tim after him. Chuck faded and faked, faded and faked, but Tim wasn't fooled. Before Chuck could throw the pass, Tim was on top of him, whacking him to the ground for a loss.

The teams lined up again. Tim dug in at the line. Again Cliff snapped the ball to Chuck. Again Tim tore into the backfield. He whacked past Updike, shoving the new tackle flat on his back. He smashed straight into Sammy Swift and he felt Sammy slide away to the side. Chuck handed the ball to Hawkins and Tim dived low at the big fullback's ankles. Tim's hands wrapped around the ankles and Tim's shoulder smacked into Hawkins' knees. The heavy fullback tumbled to the ground.

Play after play, Tim drove into the first team backfield, smearing the players for loss after loss. He could not be stopped. He banged Updike over every time. He tackled Chuck for long losses. He smashed Hawkins to the ground. He even managed to trap Sammy Swift and run the fast halfback out of bounds.

On offense, Tim was great, too. Time after time he blocked low and hard. He sent Billy flying, he hit Cliff so hard he could almost hear Cliff's teeth rattle. They were all his friends, but not today. Not when he was playing football against them.

Tim's team ran back into their huddle. They needed three yards for a first down. "Run right over me," Tim

said. "I will knock those guys away. Just follow me with
the ball and we will get a first down."

The quarterback looked up in surprise. He had never
seen Tim so full of confidence before. "Okay," he said.
"Fullback smash over tackle."

The players ran out of the huddle. Tim lined up and
looked at Billy. Tim had to knock Billy out of the play
so the fullback could get through.

The quarterback called the signals and the center
snapped the ball. Tim lunged forward and threw himself
at Billy's feet. Behind him, Tim heard the big fullback

thundering into the line. Tim hit Billy squarely, knocking him to the ground. Tim twisted around in the dirt and looked up. Sure enough, the fullback had come pounding over tackle for the first down. Tim felt great.

Tim's uniform was crusted with dirt. He was playing football the way a tackle has to play football, tough and furious. He was on the ground on every play, blocking, tackling, showing everybody that he wanted to become the best tackle who ever lived.

When Coach Bronco's whistle blew, calling an end to the day's practice, Tim wasn't even tired. He could have played for another hour. His muscles were hard and alive with the great feeling of football contact. His helmet felt light as a feather on his head.

He ran back to the locker room. He knew he had played well. He was whistling as he ran. He ran into the locker room and ripped off his helmet. He hung it on the end of the bench and just stood still for a while, feeling tough and happy.

Soon he was surrounded. Chuck was there. Billy was there. So were Jug Lary, Cliff Zanger and Sammy Swift. "You were great," Chuck said. "You were just great."

"You hit me once," Sammy said, "I felt like I was coming apart."

Jack Gerard came over, too. "Don't ever transfer schools," Jack said. "I would hate to play against you in a real game. You might kill me." The stumpy guard whacked Tim's back.

"Boswell! Boswell, get over here!"

It was Coach Bronco. He was standing at the door of the locker room. His voice was booming, and his face was twisted into a frown.

"Boswell," Coach Bronco said. "I have only one thing to say to you."

Tim bit hard on his lip. He stared into Coach Bronco's face. Suddenly the coach's face split with a big grin. "I have only one thing to say to you, Boswell," Coach Bronco said. "You are back on the first team."

## chapter 11

# TIM TO THE RESCUE

Yellow and red flames shot into the sky. They were rising high from a fire piled with logs. Cheer leaders turned somersaults. Coach Bronco bounced up and looked down from the platform at the students. Tim could hear every word the coach was saying.

"We can win tomorrow," Coach Bronco shouted. "I know that we can win."

The cheers rolled from the students around the fire. Thundering claps went with the cheers.

Coach Bronco waved his hand at the crowd, but he couldn't quiet anyone. Finally, he waved with both hands, palms down.

"We can win tomorrow," he said, his voice booming out. "We can win tomorrow if we all play together."

Coach Bronco turned toward his team. "Are we going to play together, team?" he yelled.

The whole team was on its feet. "Yes, coach," they boomed, as though they had one voice.

Coach Bronco turned to the crowd. "Okay," he yelled. "Tomorrow we beat Woodside."

The crowd began to roar. The cheers and yells cut across the night. "State U. State U. Rah-rah-rah."

Tim tumbled down the stairs behind Billy Wilson. The rest of the team was behind Tim. Jack was dancing toward the fire, taking short, choppy steps. "Snake dance," he yelled. "Snake dance."

Jack began to dance an Indian war dance around the fire. The other players danced behind him, yelling, "Beat Woodside. Beat Woodside. Beat Woodside." Soon everybody was shouting: "Beat Woodside. Beat Woodside. Beat Woodside."

Jack leaped in the air. He let loose with an Indian war yell. The State U. freshmen were on the war path to beat Woodside.

Carol turned a somersault, her bright hair glowing from the light of the fire. She flipped over, then stood up straight, then led a cheer, "State U. State U. Rah-rah-rah." The students cheered and their voices carried into the night.

It was growing darker and the yellow and red flames blazed brighter.

The cheers were ringing in Tim's ears. "We are going

122

to beat Woodside," he said to himself. "And that is a promise from me to me."

By eight o'clock, the fire was almost burned out. Carol climbed up on the platform. "One more cheer," she said, "and the meet is over."

The cheer rocked through the night, shaking everybody with its wild noise. The meet was over. The students and players were off, some to study, some to go out on dates, all to think about the big game.

Tim walked up to the platform. Carol was still standing there. She straightened her white skirt and green sweater. She looked down at Tim, smiling.

"Jump," he said.

Carol hesitated a second, then stepped off the platform. Tim's strong arms went around her as he caught her. He put her gently on the ground.

"The team has to be in bed by ten o'clock tonight," he said. "How about a walk into town for a sandwich?"

"Sure," Carol said. "But we have to get back on time. You have to get a lot of sleep for the game tomorrow."

"Don't you worry about that," Tim said. "I will be ready to tear Woodside apart with my bare hands."

They walked down the lane, circled around the library, and went along the black tar road to town. In ten minutes they were on city streets, walking to the Sugar Shop.

The lights of the Sugar Shop flickered on and off as Carol and Tim walked up to it. A brown and red turkey was painted on the frosted glass door. "It is almost

Thanksgiving," Tim said. "Boy, the months have been flying by."

Tim tugged the door open and held it while Carol walked in. Pounding, loud music roared through the room, coming from the shiny record player next to the soda fountain. Young people from the town were snapping their fingers to the music, some dancing.

Tim and Carol circled the dancers and weaved among the tables toward the back of the shop. "A lot of town kids are in here," Tim said. "I sure hope there is no trouble tonight."

"Speaking of trouble," Carol said, "look who is sitting up near the record player."

Tim slid into a booth and looked up. Len Hawkins was sitting next to a tall, brown-haired girl who was in Tim's history class. "I am not worried about Hawkins," Tim said. "It is the town kids. They started a couple of fights last week with boys from the college."

"I didn't know that," Carol said. She twisted a straw and looked at Tim.

"But nobody is likely to start one with football players," he said, smiling, and sat up as tall as he could in his seat.

"I don't know," Carol said, still twisting the straw. "There are about ten of them and they like to fight when they have more kids on their side."

"Sorry I even brought it up," Tim said. "Let's order our sandwiches."

The record player suddenly stopped. For about five seconds all was quiet. But a booming voice ended that. "One more wise crack and I will let you have it."

Tim looked up. It was Hawkins. The big fullback was on his feet, plunging into the middle of the town crowd. Tim leaped up and pulled Carol out of her seat. "Get outside," he said. "I will meet you there."

Carol looked up at Tim. He shoved her toward the door. Silently and swiftly she walked away.

Tim was watching Hawkins and the boys at the record player. The boys were moving around the big fullback, pointing their fingers at him.

"Big football player," they yelled, their voices shattering through the Sugar Shop. "Big football player. Can you fight, big football player? Or are you chicken?"

They all looked alike to Tim, their hair cropped, their faces mean. They wore black jackets. Hawkins was standing his ground, his face red, his fists doubled.

"He sure isn't afraid," Tim thought, "but if he fights, he is going to be in trouble at school."

Tim looked toward the door. He saw that it was half opened and that Carol and the tall, brown-haired girl who had been with Hawkins, were looking in, their worried faces white in the doorway.

Tim was right next to the town boys now. Suddenly he shoved through them and stood at Hawkins' side. The pack backed off for a second, not sure of themselves now that the two football players were standing side by side.

Tim looked at Hawkins. "Try not to start anything," Tim said. "If we get into trouble in town, we may be off the team."

"Hey," one of the boys yelled. "Another chicken, too. Two big, tough football players and both chicken."

Hawkins stepped toward the boy. Tim held his arm. "What are you going to prove?" Tim said. "We can wipe the floor with these guys, but so what? Let's save it for the game tomorrow. We can take it out on Woodside."

The town boys were singing together now. "Two tough football players, chicken, chicken!"

Again Hawkins moved forward and again Tim caught him. Tim held fast to the big fullback's arm and steered him toward the door. Carol had the door open as they approached it, and Tim pushed Hawkins through it.

"Thanks," Hawkins muttered. Then the big fullback turned on his heels and walked into the night. His date walked after him.

"He is one strange guy," Tim said. "He is still angry at me for something I never did."

Carol smiled. "Don't worry about him," she said. "Some day he will find out."

Hand in hand, Tim and Carol walked toward State U. Tim left her at the freshman girls' dormitory. "I will see you tomorrow," he said. "We will see each other on the field."

"Good luck," Carol said. "I know you will play well. I just know we are going to win."

Tim walked back to his dormitory, whistling and thinking hard about beating Woodside. Chuck was asleep when Tim came into the room and Tim walked quietly around, getting ready for bed. A loud knock echoed through the quiet room.

Chuck leaped out of bed, rubbing the sleep from his eyes. "What time is it?" he said. "What was that?"

Tim looked at the clock. "It is only nine-forty," Tim said. "That was the door."

"Who is it?" Chuck yelled.

"It's me, Len Hawkins. Is that you, Chuck? Can I see you?"

Chuck looked at Tim. "I had better go out," Chuck

said to Tim. "I don't want any trouble between you guys the night before the big game."

"Okay," Tim whispered.

"Wait a minute," Chuck yelled. "I am coming right out."

Chuck threw on his robe and walked out into the hall. Tim had stretched out in bed, arms crossed behind his head. Through the half open door he heard Hawkins tell Chuck in a rough whisper about the trouble in the Sugar Shop.

"Boy, the trouble I was about to get into!" Hawkins said, "but Tim stepped in before I could start anything. You know, Chuck, that is what I wanted to talk to you about. Tim must be a pretty nice guy to help me after all the trouble I have been making for him. But I don't understand one thing. How come he didn't tell me when he found out that the history examination had been changed?"

"He never knew it was changed," Chuck said. "He really never knew. He just passed it by staying up half the night studying."

Suddenly, Tim was out of bed. He threw the door open wide, and stared into Hawkins' face.

"That is the truth, Len," Tim said, "that is what happened. I stayed up to study. I never knew the test had been changed."

Hawkins looked at Tim and then back at Chuck. Suddenly, he smiled. "After the way you helped me out tonight, I would be a dope not to believe you. I am sorry I made so much trouble for you."

Hawkins held out his hand. Tim took it and they shook firmly.

"Come on into the room," Tim said. "We can talk a few minutes."

The three boys walked in and flopped down on the beds. Tim turned on the switch and the ceiling light sent a glare down into the center of the blue rug.

Hawkins stared at the light. "You know," he said, "that is what I should have done."

"What is that?" Tim said.

"Stayed up all night studying."

Tim leaned back on his pillow. "Len," he said, "do you still want to get by the easy way? Are you still playing the angles?"

"No. Believe it or not, I am not a complete dope. I learned my lesson that first week. I knew I couldn't take a chance not passing. At the time, getting those answers did seem like a smart thing, but I have learned that the risk I was taking was not worth the few hours I saved by not studying. And more important, I decided that I am in college to learn as well as to play football. I think I want to play professional football when I graduate and even in professional football, I had better know how to study. Did you ever see a professional player's book of plays?"

"Two hundred pages of plays?" Tim asked.

Hawkins nodded.

"You haven't by any chance been talking to Professor Billings, have you?" Tim asked.

"I sure have," Len said, "and he knows what he is talking about."

Tim laughed. "Well, teacher's pet."

"Don't rub it in," Len said.

A serious look came over Tim's face. "You know, Len, it was a lucky thing for Hans that you happened to be on hand the night he fell into that ditch. I saw what happened."

Len's face turned red when he heard this. "It *was* a good thing. You know I was all wrong about Hans. I know now how easy it is to make fun of people who are different, and how wrong it is, too." He looked down at his hands.

Chuck suddenly cut in. "You can just about make it back to your room by ten o'clock," he said. "We have a game tomorrow, fellows. We need all the sleep we can get."

"Right," Hawkins agreed, standing up. He walked over to Tim and the two boys shook hands again.

"Tomorrow we all play together," Chuck said, as Hawkins walked out the door. "Better than we ever played together before!"

## chapter 12

# "ANYTHING GOES IN·THE BIG GAME"

The State U. stadium was packed. Pennants were flying. The band was playing, the bass drums booming. The cheer leaders were turning somersaults at the edge of the field.

Tim stood on the field, staring into the stands. "Biggest crowd I ever saw," he said to himself. "With the varsity not playing today, everybody is here for our game." Tim pulled his helmet down tight on his head and tapped his shoulder pads. He couldn't wait for the game to begin.

Tim looked toward the goal line. He saw Hans standing off in a corner at the end of the field. And there was Carol, in front of the stands, clapping and cheering. He looked into the stands for his parents, for Terry, and for Professor Billings. He couldn't spot them, but he knew they were there. All he could see were waves of people and bright green banners. "Beat Woodside," the banners announced in big, bold letters.

At last the whistle blew. State U. and Woodside ran out and lined up for the kick off. Drums boomed and bugles sounded. Cheers rolled down from the stands.

State U. kicked off. Hawkins placed the ball on the State 40-yard line. The other ten State U. players lined up in a row, five on each side of the ball. Hawkins stepped back to the 35-yard line and began to run, ready to kick the ball. The drums sounded, banging faster and faster as he came closer to the ball. Boom! The ball was in the air, flying high, end over end, deep into Woodside territory.

Tim tore down the field, running hard, dodging Woodside players. The Woodside left halfback plucked the ball out of the air and began to run with it, faking, digging up dirt with his shoes. He dodged past Billy. He cut around Cliff. He came straight toward Tim. Tim made a dive for the player, his hands grasping for the halfback's ankles. Tim's grip began to slip. Suddenly, Jack Gerard was there, whacking the Woodside halfback with a shoulder tackle. Together Tim and Jack pounded him to the ground.

Woodside was a fast team, a team that knew what it was doing. Tim could see that. The Woodside players seemed cock sure. He heard the clear confidence in the

Woodside quarterback's voice as he barked out the signals for the next play.

Tim set himself firmly in his three-point position. He saw the ball move from the center to the quarterback to the left halfback. The halfback faked one way and ran around end, coming fast toward Tim's side of the line. Suddenly, Tim was on the ground, a pain shooting through his side. He had been hit with an elbow. He looked at the boy who had blocked him. It was the Woodside right end, the player with whom Tim would come in contact most during the game. "This is going to be rough," Tim thought, rubbing his side.

It went right on being rough, the roughest Tim had ever played in his life. Time after time all through the first half, the Woodside end hit Tim with elbows, knees and shoes. "That guy is really giving me the business," he said to Chuck.

"Stay calm," Chuck said. "Stay calm. If you get excited, you might make a mistake that will cost us the game. Keep your mind on the game, not on that end."

Neither State U. nor Woodside could score a point. This was a game of defense—hard, tough, thumping defense. The tougher it got, the more the Woodside end hit Tim with every trick in the book. Late in the third quarter, Tim dived in low to block and the Woodside end drove a knee hard and high into Tim's stomach.

Tim sank to the ground and lay there with the breath knocked out of him. Slowly he pulled himself to his feet, his face dark as night. Without saying a word, Tim stormed up to the player, his hands balled into fists. But, in that second, someone rushed between them. It was Hawkins. He forced the Woodside end farther away, so that Tim could not reach him. Then he turned and looked at Tim.

"No, Tim," he said. "Throw a punch and you will be out. Hold your temper. We need you if we are going to win."

Tim stared at Hawkins. He stared at the Woodside end. "What's the matter?" the Woodside end said. "Don't you know that anything goes in a big game like this?"

Tim turned around and walked toward the huddle, rubbing his hand against his dirty face.

"Don't worry," Chuck said. "We will get them. We have our end-around pass play. That will go. That will go for a touchdown."

"Save it," Hawkins said. "Save it for later. Save it for the big surprise."

Still nobody scored. The stands were rocking with cheers. The longer the game went on, the more the crowd cheered.

Now there were only three minutes left in the game. And Woodside had the ball. Tears of anger were streaming down Jack Gerard's dirty face. "Maybe we waited too long," the stumpy guard said. "We may not get the ball again. I don't want to have to tie these guys. I want to beat them. We have to beat them."

Tim lined up, ready to charge fast and hard. Behind him, he heard the command of Cliff Zanger. The right line backer barked, "Red dog right."

The Woodside center snapped the ball and Cliff came charging past Tim. Cliff dived for the quarterback, but the quarterback dodged him and faked a pass. It was a great fake, his arm pumping as though he were actually throwing the ball. But suddenly, in a beautiful hand-off play, he shoved the ball into the stomach of Woodside's fast left halfback.

In an instant, the halfback was tearing through the line, running right toward the position that Cliff had left

135

open. "Get him!" the State U. fans screamed. "Don't let him get loose! Get him!"

Tim was waiting. He hadn't been faked out of position. He was exactly where he was supposed to be on the red dog play, waiting for the man with the ball. He braced himself and smashed his shoulder into the halfback's knees. He wrapped his arms around the halfback and whacked him to the ground. It was a smashing tackle. The halfback couldn't hold the ball. He let go of it as he crashed to the ground and the ball went flying loose into the air. Fumble!

Jack Gerard came tearing toward the football. The stumpy guard was running as fast as he had ever run in his life. He leaped and flopped on the football. The whistle sounded through the cold November air. Recovered fumble! State U. had the ball!

Jack leaped up, waving his fist in the air. He whacked Tim on the back. "What a tackle," he said. "What a tackle, Tim. You knocked that ball right out of his hand."

Tim ran toward the huddle. He was on his way to becoming a good tackle. "I did it," he thought. "I finally did it!"

Chuck barked out the play as the State U. team gathered around him. "Now is the time," he said. "The end-around pass play."

State U. lined up on its own 40-yard line. They had a long way to go to cover the sixty yards to the goal line. Cliff bent over the ball at the center. Jack and Tim dug in at the line. Billy was ready to race back for the ball. Chuck was behind Cliff, shouting out the signals.

"Set! Down! Blue white. Got it. One, two. . . ."

Cliff snapped the ball. Chuck grabbed it and faded back. Sammy Swift ran past Chuck and cut down the field, turning on every ounce of speed at his command.

Billy Wilson came circling back from his end position. Tim banged low and hard into the Woodside end, pounding him out of the play. There was Sammy on the Woodside 20-yard line and free as any football player could ever be.

Billy drew back his arm and let loose a long pass. It went flying down the field. Woodside had been fooled, but the pass was going over Sammy Swift's head. Sammy ran still faster and, at the very last instant, he made a dive toward the football. His hands reached out as far as they could go and they grabbed the ball. Sammy slid on his stomach, but he had caught the ball and he was on the Woodside 15-yard line. The end-around pass play had worked!

The State U. students were going wild in the stands. They were cheering and clapping, stamping on the wooden seats, and whacking each other on the back. What a play! What a great play!

Tim looked up at the clock. There were twenty seconds left. State U. had time for either two passing plays or one running play. The clock would stop on a passing play that was not complete, but was it worth the risk?

Chuck, the quarterback, decided to play it safe. Quickly, he called the signal. "Fullback smash. Straight up the middle," he said. "Hawkins, it is up to you."

Cliff bent over the ball. Chuck lined up behind him, barking out the play. "Set! Down! Got it! Three straight! One, two, three. . . ."

Cliff snapped the ball and Tim smashed forward. Chuck slapped the ball in Hawkins' stomach and the big fullback came rushing forward. Tim drove hard and straight at the Woodside end, knocking him out of Hawkins' path with a brush block.

Hawkins came blasting through the hole with Tim right in front of him. The big fullback's head was down, his legs were whirling, his shoes were kicking up dirt. Tim was pounding along, fast and furious, in front of him.

Now Hawkins was at the 5-yard line. Then he was at the 4-yard line. Billy belted the Woodside line backer away. Jack whacked the Woodside halfback to the ground. Only the safety man remained. Only the safety man stood between Hawkins and the goal line.

Now Tim moved straight toward the safety man. The safety man faked with his feet and shoulders, but Tim wasn't fooled. Tim had his eyes on the safety man's hips and flew low and hard at his ankles. Tim's shoulder smashed into the safety man's legs. Hawkins thundered past him, over the goal line.

Touchdown! The winning touchdown! State U. had

won! The big game was over, and State U. had won.

Banners flew down from the stands. Carol and the other cheer leaders danced up and down, screaming themselves hoarse, turning somersaults. The State U. students came pouring down on the field. Some were tugging at the goal posts, others were pounding the players on the backs.

The speaker boomed. "Will you please clear the field so that State U. can kick the extra point. The game is over, but State U. can still kick the extra point."

Nobody listened. Who cared? Who needed the extra point? Jack and Jug were hugging each other. Chuck and Billy and Sammy Swift were leaping up and down. The cheers were loud and happy.

Tim was running toward the locker room. Coach Bronco slapped him on the back. "Great game, Boswell," he boomed.

Tim looked behind him. There was Hawkins, being lifted up on the shoulders of the State U. students. They were singing and shouting. "Hurrah for Hawkins. Hurrah for Hawkins."

The State U. students were coming on the field from all sides. They were all over the field, running and jumping and cheering. Tim was pushed back by the crowd, toward the center of the field. He was right next to Hawkins. Then Hawkins leaped from the students' shoulders. He jumped down next to Tim.

"They should be holding you up on their shoulders,"

Hawkins said. "You got me over for that touchdown, Tim. You are the one they should be cheering."

Tim flipped his helmet high in the air. He rubbed his sore side and ran the sleeve of his white jersey across his dirty face.

Suddenly, his face split with a big grin. "You carried the ball, Len, so you take the cheers for all of us. And you know something," he added. "I have a feeling that you and I are going to be winning football games and hearing cheers at State U. for a long, long time."